W9-BUI-797

Mystery in Mt. Mole

Mystery in Mt. Mole

Richard W. Jennings

Houghton Mifflin Company Boston 2003

Walter Lorraine Books

NEW HANOVER COUNTY PUBLIC LIBRARY
201 Chestnut Street
Wilmington, NC 28401

Acknowledgment: The author thanks the Kansas Arts Commission and Smith Lamar & Associates, Fairway, Kansas, for their contributions toward the completion of this book.

Walter Lorraine (wл) Books

Copyright © 2003 by Richard W. Jennings

All rights reserved. For information about permission to reproduce selections from this book, write to Permissions, Houghton Mifflin Company, 215 Park Avenue South, New York, New York 10003.

www.houghtonmifflinbooks.com

Library of Congress Cataloging-in-Publication Data

Jennings, Richard W. (Richard Walker), 1945-
  Mystery in Mt. Mole / Richard W. Jennings.
      p. cm.
Summary: While twelve-year-old Andrew J. Forrest searches for Mr. Farley, the very unpopular assistant principal at Mt. Mole Middle School, strange things are happening on the town's namesake hill.
  ISBN 0-618-28478-8
  [1. City and town life—Great Plains—Fiction. 2. Volcanoes—Fiction. 3. Great Plains—Fiction. 4. Mystery and detective stories.] I. Title.
  PZ7J4298765Myf 2003
  [Fic]--dc21
                                                            2003000534

Printed in the United States of America
MP 10 9 8 7 6 5 4 3 2 1

To Carol Jennings Powell

Mystery in Mt. Mole

Vanished!

Mr. Farley was missing. Have no doubt about that.

His disappearance was reported in the *Weekly Mountain Chronicle,* and unless you're the sort of person who tends to confuse one frowning face with another, the photograph on the front page made it crystal clear: It was Assistant Principal Farley, all right. He was as missing as a snail's toenail.

And while as chief disciplinarian of Mt. Mole Middle School, Mr. Farley was far and away its most unpopular person, in my opinion, even *he* did not deserve what may have been perpetrated by persons, beings, or forces unknown.

Unfortunately, there was no eyewitness to the incident. There was, however, a reliable *ear*witness—namely me. I'd just stepped onto Mr. Farley's front porch to present some after-school detention papers for his signature when I heard a sound like distant shots coming from his living room, followed by Mr. Farley's voice crying out, "Oh, no!"

Uh, oh! I thought, diving into the bushes. *Maybe I should come back later.*

But curiosity, as many an injured cat will tell you, is a powerful force. After waiting an appropriate interval, I entered Mr. Farley's house, where, lying on the floor in front of his television, I discovered not Mr. Farley, but Mr. Farley's tattersall plaid pajamas peeking out from underneath a mountain of butter-flavored popcorn.

"It was enough popcorn," I told the reporter from the *Weekly Mountain Chronicle,* "to pack a set of china."

Needless to say, the police were baffled. I say "needless to say," because everyone who lives in the town of Mt. Mole knows that the Mt. Mole Volunteer Police Department is no more capable of solving a real crime than the man in the moon. The only reason Chief Eagle Talon got the job was because everybody was already accustomed to calling him "Chief."

Despite the facts being unknown, some of the residents of Mt. Mole expressed alarm, not because they'd lost anyone they cared about, but because the town prided itself on its violent crime–free record.

Come live in Mt. Mole, the Chamber of Commerce brochure promised, *and you'll die of natural causes.*

"Why, heck," complained Mr. Knott, the business group's president, "we've still got two full boxes of those things."

I was concerned for other reasons. The sudden loss of the assistant principal had resulted in the temporary closing of the school. Tedious though it sometimes was, without the daily diversion provided by my teachers and classmates, there was little to look forward to in Mt. Mole.

Someone, I realized, would have to solve the mystery. Since the investigative talent pool in this tiny prairie town was pretty shallow, that someone, I supposed, would have to be me.

Permit me to introduce myself. My name is Andrew J. Forrest. The middle initial doesn't stand for anything, my mother explained long ago. It's just there, like the solitary "S" in President Harry S. Truman's name. Anyway, my full name hardly matters, because everybody in Mt. Mole just calls me "Andy." I'm very nearly thirteen years old — so close, in fact, that I may as well go ahead and claim it.

Responding to a persistent, nagging sensation, like an itch inside a sock, I decided to begin my investigation of Mr. Farley's disappearance by revisiting the scene of the crime.

"I'm going out, Irene," I called to my mother. "I'll be back later."

Getting around Mt. Mole is easy, especially if you have a new battery-powered scooter, as I did. The place is not only as flat as a checkerboard, it's laid out like one, too, with all the east-west streets numbered sequentially, and the north-south streets bearing the names of native animals, arranged alphabetically.

For example, until recently, my mother and I lived in a house at the corner of Ninth and Muskrat. Now we're ten blocks away, in the Lucius Knott Blue Ribbon Inn, where Toad Street meets the state highway. My mother works in the business district, a hodgepodge of buildings huddled around Third Street, from Porcupine to Butterfly. The middle school is located on Twelfth Street, halfway between Groundhog and Heron. The house that Mr. Farley rented is at Tenth and Flea. I could draw you a map, but the point is this: In Mt. Mole, no matter where you happen to find yourself, you're never far from where you need to be.

The house where Assistant Principal Farley disappeared was at least a hundred years old. Dark-shuttered dormers hung like gargoyles from its steeply pitched roof. A wide wooden porch, framed with thick, squat columns, wrapped all the way from the back to the frosted glass door in the front.

Nobody was around, so like any other detective

4

worth his salt, I let myself in. Anyway, it's not like it was breaking and entering. Strictly speaking, it was just entering, which in Mt. Mole—where doors are left unlocked and it's considered rude to make someone wait outside even if you aren't home—is more or less the custom. Nor was it strange to find a crime scene open to the public, so to speak. Chief Eagle Talon didn't put much faith in the analysis of clues. To solve the handful of crimes that came his way each year, the Chief relied on his psychic powers.

"It's as reliable as any other method," he explained, "and often can be accomplished while napping."

The only thing to suggest something unusual had happened at Mr. Farley's house was a duct-taped X on the floor in front of the television marking the spot where I'd found the popcorn-covered pajamas. Other than that, the place was just as Mr. Farley had left it—as neat as a pin and twice as sharp.

On a bookshelf, travel magazines organized by date filled neat rows of matching cardboard holders. Framed photographs—dozens of them—stood edge to edge across the top, each one depicting Assistant Principal Farley in front of a world-famous building or landmark. Silently, I studied the images, noting that in all of them, Mr. Farley was alone. Nor were there pictures of other people anywhere else in the room—not even a snapshot of a dog or cat. Perhaps, I reasoned, this explained why in every picture Mr. Farley's face displayed the beginnings of a frown.

Interesting, I thought. *It's like the* Mona Lisa *turned upside down.*

The mysterious half-frown belonged to a man apparently near the middle of his allotted years, a man of slightly less than average height, with a thinning, light brown head of hair approximately the color of my own and a large, rosy, Romanesque nose. Upon this prominent feature was balanced a pair of thick, black-framed glasses — an especially unfortunate style, in my opinion, since they gave Mr. Farley the appearance of a person wearing a novelty shop disguise. With such an exaggerated, standoffish appearance, and a reputation for a fiery temper and little patience for the opinions of others, it's no wonder that few people in Mt. Mole liked Mr. Farley.

And yet, I thought, seeing his pictures in the light of his mysterious disappearance, *I can't help but feel there's something about the man I've overlooked.*

Satisfied that circumstances justified my snooping, I continued my search in the kitchen. Here I found Mr. Farley's dishes grouped according to pattern and color, and his canned goods, bags, and boxes organized by type and size.

Such a neat and tidy man, I thought.

Indeed, the primary difference between the appearance of Mr. Farley's house and that of a home furnishings store was that fact that there was an absence of instrumental music coming from the ceiling.

Upstairs, in the bedroom closet, Mr. Farley's suits hung in separate plastic bags from the Mt. Mole One-Day Laundry Cleaners. In the bathroom cabinet, skin care, dental care, and shaving supplies were stored in color-coded Tupperware containers.

Even Mr. Farley's trash was carefully arranged. In a pegboard-lined storage closet, I found newspapers bundled chronologically; food cartons flattened, color-sorted, and placed inside grocery bags; plastic bottles, glass jars, and discarded mail sorted, stacked, and secured as if it were being carefully cataloged for a museum.

Hmmm, I thought. *Unlike me, this is a man who requires order.*

For such a person, a messy living room seemed quite out of character.

The living room is the first room in the house that visitors typically see, yet for some reason, Mr. Farley's living room floor was strewn with plaid pajamas, popcorn, empty packages, and many other odds and ends, including, now that I thought about it, an obviously expensive graphing calculator. Returning to the crime scene, I also found a number of boxes from the town's only movie rental store, Hollywood Meets Mt. Mole, located at the corner of Third and Dog.

Picking up a movie called *Curse of the Slime Creature,* I examined the cover. It featured an illustration of a snarling, vine-covered, half-human form dragging a limp victim through the mud.

"Ugh!" I exclaimed with a shudder.

I sifted through the other titles: *Vampire Spiders from Outer Space; Attack of the Zombie Rats; Invasion of the Ferret People.*

My gosh! I thought. *Did Mr. Farley fall victim to alien forces?*

Suddenly, it occurred to me that the movie Mr. Farley was watching when he departed so abruptly might still be in the player. I pushed the power button. The tray slid open to present a silver disk. Squinting at its mirrored surface, I read the title: *Highlights of the International Conference on Vulcanology.*

Good grief! I thought.

Noting that all the movies were marked "Two-Evening Rental," I did some quick calculations in my head. Mr. Farley had disappeared on a Friday afternoon. This was Monday.

Uh-oh, I thought. *If these aren't returned soon, Mr. Farley's going to owe a fortune in late charges!*

No Friend of Farley's

In the absence of a plan, I figured, the best thing is to simply follow your nose. Who knows where the path might lead? My search of Mr. Farley's house had turned up a curious collection of movies. Perhaps more clues were waiting at the movie rental store.

Sharing a white-brick building with a pet-grooming salon and a Polynesian-style restaurant, Hollywood Meets Mt. Mole was a dusty, cluttered shop with all the ambiance of an unheated garage. On the walls, faded posters from long-forgotten films dangled from rusted thumbtacks. Sagging card tables strained under the weight of hundreds of haphazardly arranged movies, piled up like underwear in a dresser drawer. But the store had neither customers nor employees when I entered and, judging by the acrid aroma that filled the room and the blackened carafe of an electric coffeemaker in the corner, it had been that way all morning.

I tapped a bell on the counter. When no one came, I tapped again. Once more I waited. Finally, after a musical burst of seven taps in a row, the proprietor, a harried-looking woman with drawn-on eyebrows, emerged from the back with a wet, suds-covered, nearly toothless dog in her arms.

"Yes?" she asked, her voice betraying annoyance until she recognized me. "Oh, hello, Andy."

"Hi, Mrs. Stitch," I said, holding up the movies. "I'm bringing these back."

"Just put them on the table, will you?" she said, struggling to keep the dripping dog from sliding to the floor.

"Sure," I replied. "But just so you know, they're

not mine. I'm pretty sure they were rented by Mr. Farley."

The movie store proprietor's face took on a stricken look, as if she'd suddenly bitten down on a bad lima bean. Could it have been because I'd mentioned Mr. Farley? Or was it only a reaction to the soggy pooch in her arms?

I continued to probe.

"Isn't it terrible?" I said, shaking my head. "Poor Mr. Farley."

"Good riddance, if you ask me," Mrs. Stitch snapped. "Farley was a real horse's patoot. Why, compared to him, my ex-husband had charm."

"But Mr. Farley was a customer of yours, wasn't he?" I asked.

"If they want to rent a movie," Mrs. Stitch replied, dumping the old dog on the floor, where he lay like a discarded towel, "everybody in Mt. Mole is a customer of mine. That doesn't automatically make them likable. Farley was an especially disagreeable man. Even the daily double wasn't good enough for him."

"The daily double?" I repeated.

"My latest sales-promotion idea," Mrs. Stitch explained proudly. "Every day, I come up with a different special offer to bring in customers. Saturday's daily double was rent two movies and, for only two dollars more, get a two-liter bottle of diet cola and two bags of butter-flavored microwave popcorn."

"Mr. Farley didn't like that?" I responded, surprised. "That's a great deal!"

"Oh, he liked the deal, all right," Mrs. Stitch answered, "but he demanded that I swap a family-size bag of gummy worms for the popcorn. He said popcorn gave him gas."

"That's interesting," I commented.

"Not to me, it isn't," Mrs. Stitch continued. "Anyway, I explained that I couldn't make the substitution because everything in the daily double has to have a two in it—two movies, two liters, two bags of popcorn—see? That's why it's called the daily double. But you know Farley."

"Yes," I said. "But eventually he took the popcorn, anyway, right?"

"No, as a matter of fact, he didn't," Mrs. Stitch said, shifting her weight from one foot to the other, a maneuver that caused her to step on the toes of the elderly canine.

"YIP!" the animal cried.

"Well, what did you expect, Vesuvius!" Mrs. Stitch exclaimed. "You were asking for it!"

"So what *did* Mr. Farley do?" I asked.

"He threw a fit right here in this store, that's what he did," Mrs. Stitch replied. "Picked up a bag of gummy worms and ripped it right in half! Candy was flying everywhere! In all my days, I've never seen such a thing!"

"How terrible," I said.

"It gets worse," Mrs. Stitch continued. "Glowering like some sort of madman, he puts his face right up to mine and says, 'There's your two, lady, now give me my movies!' Can you imagine, Andy? I mean to tell you! What a nasty man Mr. Farley is — or was! Why, if he hadn't already paid me in cash, I'd have sicced Chief Eagle Talon on him right then and there! The nerve of some people!"

"I guess it takes all kinds," I said.

"You're telling me," Mrs. Stitch replied, still steaming from the memory of the encounter.

"By the way," I asked, pausing as I headed toward the door, "what's today's daily double?"

Brightening visibly, the enterprising owner of the pet grooming/Polynesian restaurant/movie rental complex recited, "Wash two dogs and get two slices of squid and two Popeye cartoons for only two dollars more."

"Hmmm," I said. "Any takers?"

"Not so far," she answered, "but the lunch rush hasn't started yet."

The Investigation Intensifies

Mrs. Stitch's mention of the lunch rush reminded me that it was time to head for home.

Since my mother and I moved into the Knott Inn,

we'd been taking our meals at the Lucius Knott Hungry Family Restaurant next door. Unlike some dining establishments, this one operated on a restricted schedule, since the chef was also the desk clerk at the motel. Breakfast was served from seven until eight, lunch from noon to one, and dinner from six until seven. If you showed up late for a meal, you had to settle for something from the vending machines.

The nineteen-block trip from Third and Dog to Sixth and Toad was a breeze thanks to Pegasus, a factory-reconditioned, twenty-four-volt electric scooter that my mother bought me shortly after a tornado took our house and nearly everything in it — including my only pet, a hermit crab named Stony.

With a top speed of seventeen miles per hour, Pegasus could carry two kids or one adult up to fourteen miles or for two hours on a single charge. Shiny, black, and near-silent in operation, Pegasus was the coolest man-made object in Mt. Mole. No swimming pool, computer, or home entertainment system could have done as much for an almost-teenager's image as Pegasus did for mine. Whenever I was on Pegasus, I was on top of the world.

Fittingly, it was a beautiful spring day, without so much as a wisp of a cloud to mar the Easter-egg blue of the sky. In the distance, some two miles away, rising one hundred and sixty-five feet from a vast expanse of grassland as flat as an airport runway, was the distinctive humpback bump of Mt. Mole, the topographical curiosity from which the town of Mt. Mole took its name.

Although not large by world standards — the mountain was roughly one-third the height of the Washington Monument and half as tall as the Statue of Liberty — when seen in the center of a flat, vacant prairie, Mt. Mole seemed enormous, at least to me.

Mt. Mole's ability to attract the eye was further enhanced by the presence of Knott Grande, the lavish residence of the richest man in town, situated at the mountain's pinnacle and gleaming like a jewel in the sun. Constructed of native limestone in the style of a Spanish nobleman's castle and enlarged many times over the years, Knott Grande was first built by Francisco Vásquez de Coronado and his men, who, in their search for gold, chose this site for its magnificent view of the plains.

I'd never been there, of course. Few Mt. Moleans had.

My scoot down Third Street took me to within a couple of blocks of the historic Mt. Mole Depot. Although no longer a working train station — the railroad had given up on Mt. Mole years ago — the depot lived on as the headquarters of the Mt. Mole Society for Railroad Preservation, a group with both time and tools on their hands. Since birds of a feather tend to reminisce together, over the years, Mt. Mole Depot had become the preferred hangout of the town's senior citizens, including its chief of volunteer police, Chief Eagle Talon. Most of the time, the Chief could be found inside occupying a well-worn bench in the waiting room, chatting with his chums, reading the newspaper, or lying on his back cultivating his visions.

I took a quick dogleg right on Lizard to where a grim, two-story cinder-block building hunkers down on First Street like it's daring you to come in.

Behind the ticket counter sat a bald-headed man whose name I knew to be Earl. Tufts of white hair sprouted from his ears.

"Good morning, Earl," I said cheerfully.

"Morning," Earl mumbled.

"Is the Chief around?" I inquired. "I've got a question for him."

"Not here," Earl replied. "Working on a case."

"The Farley case?" I asked.

"What other case would it be?" Earl responded. "Amelia Earhart?"

"Who?" I asked.

"Never mind," Earl said, scratching at his ear like a basset hound with fleas. "Which," he continued, "is the same thing I told the Chief: 'Never mind.' I said. 'It's only Farley, so why bother?'"

"I take it that Mr. Farley managed to rub you the wrong way," I concluded.

"Ha, that's a good one!" Earl snorted, breaking into another round of vigorous ear massage.

I nodded my head politely and waited.

"Did you know that that fool Farley was an enemy of the trains?" Earl continued. "Said they were a symbol of, and I quote, 'the exploitation of the land and the destruction of the native people.' Said it to me while I was flat on my back under the steamer working on a pilot wheel, or else I would have decked him. 'The history of the railroads, Earl,' he said, in that smug, know-it-all way of his, 'is the history of man at his greediest. You should hang your head in shame.'"

"Strong words," I observed.

"Fighting words, as far as I'm concerned," Earl sputtered. "Why, if it weren't for the railroads, this country wouldn't even exist. Who the blazes did Farley think he was?"

"I guess he could have picked a different place to criticize the trains," I observed. "Considering all that you fellows do here."

"No kidding," Earl agreed.

"By the way," I asked, "just out of curiosity, where were you when Mr. Farley disappeared?"

Earl, however, didn't hear my question, inasmuch as both his ears were undergoing an assault from his hands.

Maybe later, I thought, as I let myself out and closed the door behind me.

I barely made it to the Knott Hungry in time. Taking my regular seat at the end of the counter, I was handed the last slice of meat loaf, a hard, rubbery end cut that shared a puddle of gravy with three pale Brussels sprouts. The mashed potatoes I'd been hoping for were being polished off by the man sitting next to me, who, coincidentally, was the very person I was seeking — Chief Eagle Talon.

"Chief," I said. "Missed you at the station."

"Andy," he attempted to reply, but with so many potatoes in his mouth it sounded more like "Mmmff."

"Sorry to bother you outside your office," I said, "but I was wondering if you'd made any progress on the Farley case."

"Nothing yet," Chief Eagle Talon answered. "But possibly the solution will come to me in a vision."

"Here's hoping," I said.

I let the Chief enjoy his meal while my eyes searched the room. The Knott Hungry was furnished in a 1950s style, not because anybody in Mt. Mole paid attention to design trends, but because no one had bothered to redecorate the place since the day it was built.

In one dark, varnished plywood booth I spotted the new family in town, Mr. and Mrs. Wayne and their twelve-year-old daughter, Georgia. Talk about bad luck! The Waynes had no sooner arrived in Mt. Mole than the tornado that snatched my house also helped itself to theirs. Now the Waynes were once again my neighbors, this time at the Knott Inn, where

17

they lived in the double rooms directly upstairs.

From this angle, I couldn't help but notice how much Georgia looked like a certain popular singer, a perky, blonde-haired teen whose latest song was always on the radio. I wondered if anybody had ever mentioned the resemblance to Georgia, and if so, how she felt about it, but at that moment, she glanced up from her plate and caught me staring. Flustered, I forced a smile and raised my glass in salute. Georgia responded with what appeared to be a blush — although from that distance, with my eyesight, I couldn't be absolutely sure. Then she gave a hesitant wave and turned away.

To the right of the Waynes, the remaining three booths were filled with their customary occupants — the familiar weathered faces of members of the Railroad Preservation Society. Opposite them, at a single table favored by Mr. Farley, was a man I didn't recognize — an unusual occurrence in a town where everybody knows everybody. Dressed in a gray three-piece suit that matched a conspicuous streak in his hair, he was eating lunch while writing in a notebook.

Hmmm, I thought. *It's unlikely he's the new food critic for the* Weekly Mountain Chronicle.

"Chief," I said, tapping my seatmate on the arm. "Do you know who that man is — the one sitting by himself beside the restrooms?"

The Chief glanced over his shoulder.

"Nope," he replied.

If I were compiling a list of suspects, I'd put that guy on it, I thought.

That was when I realized what a blunder I'd been making in my investigation. Here I was searching the town for clues and I'd failed to write down the name of a single suspect!

Rats! I thought.

Borrowing the waitress's pen, I pulled a paper napkin from the chrome holder on the table in front of me and wrote: "Suspects: Number one. Man with gray streak in hair."

Here I paused. What were my grounds for suspicion? Nothing more than that I didn't know who he was. But in an investigation where the victim was so unpopular, until the newcomer could produce a satisfactory alibi, this was enough.

"Stranger," I wrote boldly and decisively.

Then, starting a second line, I printed the words, "Number two."

Who was number two? I wondered. Did I have any other suspects?

What about Mrs. Stitch? I thought.

Mrs. Stitch had a motive. Mr. Farley had made her mad. Mrs. Stitch sold an item found at the scene — butter-flavored popcorn — and lots of it. And what was it she said to that poor old dog when she accidentally stepped on him? "You were asking for it!"

Yes, I concluded, *she's definitely a suspect.*

"Mrs. Stitch, dog groomer, restaurateur, and movie store proprietor," I wrote.

Earl was a suspect, too, I concluded, given what he claimed Mr. Farley had said about the railroads.

As I wrote Earl's name down as suspect number three, the pen wore a hole in the soft, absorbent paper.

Holy smokes! I thought. *I've barely gotten started and already I have three suspects! This case is going to require a lot of napkins!*

"Chief?" I asked, as Chief Eagle Talon lifted a forkful of banana cream pie to his lips. "If you were going to make a list of Mr. Farley's enemies, how would you go about it?"

Savoring his dessert, Chief Eagle Talon closed his eyes, swallowed, then pointed with his fork to a shelf under the counter. "There's the phone book," he said. "I'd start with the names in there."

Outside, feeling the effects of the midday meal, I stretched out my arms and yawned. High overhead, a solitary hawk soared in circles without beating a wing. Underneath this airborne athlete, on the peak of Mt. Mole, Knott Grande glistened in the prairie sun like a golden crown. Closer to home, on the deck of Pegasus, a grasshopper rubbed its spindly legs. With a flick of my fingertip, I brushed the brown intruder aside, switched on the power, and zipped up Sixth Street as ideas for solving Mt. Mole's most mysterious crime popped and skittered in my head.

Whoever is the culprit, I reasoned, *whether it's Earl, Mrs. Stitch, the stranger, or someone I haven't yet suspected, their conscience is bound to be troubling them.*

I decided to consult an expert in such matters.

Scooting past Opossum, at Nuthatch Street, on the western edge of the tornado's savage path, Pegasus and I took a left and slipped over four blocks to Second Street, to the High Hopes New Millennium Theoretical Church, where the Reverend J. Clement Oxide is pastor. I found Reverend Oxide in his office reading his e-mails and snacking his way through lunch.

"Reverend Oxide?" I spoke tentatively. "I hope I'm not interrupting."

"Andy," he greeted me. "How nice to see you."

From a silver bowl by his computer monitor, the spiritual leader removed his right hand and extended it in welcome, the practiced handshake firm, but the fingers unpleasantly greasy.

"I was just wondering," I explained, wiping my palm against my jeans, "if somebody confesses a crime to you, do you have to tell the police?"

"Well, now, that all depends," he hedged. "What have you done?"

"Oh, it isn't me," I asserted. "I'm just trying to find out if you might know what happened to Mr. Farley."

Like an actor responding to a cue, Reverend

Oxide's face struck a somber look.

"Ah," he replied. "Mr. Farley. Not exactly the most favored person in our midst — not by a long shot. He once interrupted a sermon — did you know that? Stopped me right in the middle of my description of life in the hereafter. What a dreadful man! In front of the entire congregation, he had the audacity to say — and I quote — 'The only difference between you and the bogeyman, Reverend, is your custom-tailored robe.'"

My goodness! I thought.

Reverend Oxide sighed, shook his head, and tapped at his computer keyboard. After a couple of clicks, a bite of his snack, and a swig of cola, he continued.

"In my opinion," he volunteered, "Mt. Mole is a much better place without the likes of Mr. Farley."

"But surely," I suggested, "you, of all people, should be willing to let bygones be bygones!"

Reverend Oxide wrinkled his brow. "Maybe," he confessed, "so long as what's 'gone' is not only the offensive act, but the individual in question. In any event, we'll deal with this at the town meeting."

"The town meeting?" I asked. "What town meeting is that?"

"The one I'm conducting for the Mt. Mole Chamber of Commerce," Reverend Oxide explained, "tomorrow morning, at ten o'clock, at Mt. Mole Memorial Gardens."

"But that's the cemetery!" I protested. "Mr. Farley isn't dead. He's only missing!"

For what seemed an eternity, Reverend Oxide stared at me without blinking, his blank, puzzled gaze like that of a chicken.

"In a situation like this," he said at last, "it's better to be safe than sorry. Will you be there?"

"I guess so," I replied.

"Well, then," he said. "See you tomorrow. Now, if you'll excuse me, I have an appointment on the other side of town."

Standing to put on his sports jacket, Mt. Mole's spiritual leader reached behind his computer and produced a bowl of popcorn.

"You're welcome to finish this," he offered, suppressing a burp. "It's butter-flavored."

Holy smokes! I thought. *Not him, too!*

My hands shaking with excitement, the moment I stepped outside I pulled out my tattered napkin and wrote down the Reverend's name.

Sudden Insights

I've said that in Mt. Mole everybody knows everybody — but do they?

The fact is, even in a town as tiny as Mt. Mole, people will astonish you — Mrs. Stitch, Earl, Chief Eagle Talon, Reverend Oxide, and Georgia Wayne, to name a few. Why, until Assistant Principal Farley disappeared, who knew he was such a well-organized man, interested in horror movies, international travel, and vulcanology?

When it comes to understanding one another, human beings seem poorly equipped for the task. Hawks see all there is to know about other hawks from a mile away. Dogs sniff out each other's intentions in seconds. Insects are born knowing who's supposed to be doing what, and they work harder at it than people ever will.

Rare is the person who's willing to ride a few blocks on someone else's scooter, I thought, *much less walk a mile in his shoes.*

Here's another realization that suddenly came to mind: More people are injured practicing amateur philosophy than are hurt rewiring lamps, frying donuts, and skating on thin ice — combined. That's because amateur philosophizing is virtually indistinguishable from daydreaming.

I mention this because not two seconds after I thought about how most people are too preoccupied to notice each other, Pegasus ran over the curb at First and Jackalope and I tumbled head over heels into the street, skinning my elbow, bumping my head, and losing my list of suspects in the process.

"Ow!" I cried.

Lying on the pavement, scraped and stunned, two more important truths revealed themselves: One, when riding on a scooter, always wear a helmet; and two, nothing in this life is free—we pay for every insight we receive.

As added proof, even *this* philosophical fragment was not without cost. Like the aftershock from an earthquake, Pegasus, which had been leaning precariously against the curb, suddenly succumbed to the force of gravity and fell on me—all sixty-six pounds of it.

I lay still, catching my breath, careful to allow no uninvited insights into my head, until, after an interval of several minutes, the honking of an automobile horn brought me to my feet.

Looking up, I saw a big, black, German-made sedan speeding by. As it passed, a man waved from an open window in a greeting characteristic of the Queen of England—except the Queen of England, one supposes, rarely spits tobacco juice into the street.

"Hello, Mr. Knott," I called in respectful recognition. But Mr. Knott was already gone.

I'd considered dropping in on my mother at work, but not wishing to worry her about my spill, I turned south instead, toward the Knott Inn, where I hoped to collect my thoughts and treat my skinned elbow. As I was turning right at Sixth and Jackalope, a woman with a fluffy-haired, bent-legged, nearly toothless dog crossed my path.

"Hello!" I called.

It was my English teacher and faculty adviser from Mt. Mole Middle School — Miss Futon. On any other Monday at this time of day, I'd be sitting in her classroom.

"Are you enjoying this unexpected holiday?" I asked.

Apparently this was the wrong thing to say, for no sooner had the well-intentioned words escaped my lips than Miss Futon burst into tears.

"Boo-hoo," she wailed. "Boo-hoo-hoo, sniff."

"I'm sorry," I apologized, with a sympathetic glance at her companion. "Is there something wrong with your dog?"

"What?" the red-eyed, puffy-faced Miss Futon responded. "You mean Vesuvius? Vesuvius is fine! It's Jacob I'm concerned about! Poor, poor Jacob. He's gone! Vanished like a . . . like a . . ."

Sensing that my English teacher was struggling for the perfect metaphor, possibly to describe a runaway pet, I suggested helpfully, "Like a borrowed ballpoint pen? Like the last cookie in the bag? Like the wiggle in a weasel flattened by a steam locomotive?"

"Boo-hoo! " Miss Futon bellowed. "Boo-hoo-hoo-hoo-hoo!"

Oh, man! I thought.

With a weak, embarrassed smile, I offered a half-wave of goodbye and turned Pegasus west in the direction of the Lucius Knott Blue Ribbon Inn. Crossing Kingfisher Street, I glanced back over my shoulder to see Miss Futon, her head low, trudging down the sidewalk behind her creaky old dog.

There's more to this than meets the eye, I reasoned.

Back in my room, I washed my elbow, stuck on a Band-Aid, and lay down on the king-size bed. Even though the day was only half over, I was exhausted.

On the nightstand beside me was a short stack of comic books. Once part of an extensive collection of vintage works, these few flimsy paperbound pages were among my only possessions to survive the Mt. Mole tornado. Flipping through their familiar images, I marveled at how the artist, relying on improbable plots, exaggerated situations, unlikely coincidences, and an ensemble of wisecracking characters distinguished from each other by such superficial attributes as the shape of their ears or the color of their hats, had managed to draw such an insightful picture of life.

More often than not, I mused, *this is the way things are.*

Chuckling at the antics of a trio of jailbird dogs whose plan to kidnap a wealthy old duck had gone awry for the umpteenth time, I wondered if something like this might have happened to Mr. Farley. Had he been nabbed by a gang of crooks? But why? If simply being obnoxious were reason to be kidnapped, none of us would be safe in our homes.

But Mr. Farley wasn't like the rest of us, I was learning. He had a special knack for irritating people in the extreme. He fought with nearly everyone who crossed his path—coworkers, neighbors, store clerks, strangers on the phone. Apparently, something deep inside Mr. Farley burned hotter than it does in other people.

I'd seen evidence of this firsthand. I recall one Sunday afternoon in particular. I was at Mt. Mole Pharmacy & Gifts, shopping for a comic book, when I was startled by someone shouting.

"You don't know what you're talking about, sister," an angry voice declared, "and the more you flap those fat lips of yours, the more you reveal your ignorance!"

Cautiously, I peeked through a snack food display to see who was causing such a commotion. It was Mr. Farley, of course. He was shaking his finger in the frightened face of a woman I recognized as the weekend assistant manager. At issue, it seemed, was a roll of film from Mr. Farley's travels that the store had somehow ruined.

Taking pity on the woman, another customer tried to intervene, but Mr. Farley would have none of it. He began raging at the interloper, as well, advising her that she was "about as welcome as a case of boils and every bit as attractive."

Soon, half a dozen customers were involved in the fracas, none of them sympathetic to Mr. Farley even though he was the one who'd suffered harm in the first place. He had the facts on his side, but not the people.

"Pinheads!" Mr. Farley shouted, storming out of the store. "This whole stinking town is populated by pinheads!"

I didn't take his words personally. I figured he couldn't help it. For some reason, Mr. Farley was a slave to his own bad temper. But I could certainly understand why other people might dislike him—a lot.

Let's face it, I reasoned. *Anybody in Mt. Mole could be behind Mr. Farley's disappearance.*

Responding to a sudden chill, I pulled the motel's rubbery blanket around me, an action that flipped the television remote control to the floor. When the screen popped on and a man's voice asked, "Will it ever rain again in Mt. Mole?" my heart performed a somersault.

Get hold of yourself, Andy! I thought. *It's just a weather report.*

Although I'm practically thirteen years old and am often required to take care of myself, I've never been good at it. Sometimes, I get the willies when I'm alone.

When my mother tapped on the door between our rooms to let me know that she'd returned, it was well after five o'clock. Soon, we were crossing the parking lot to the Knott Hungry. The sun, sinking into the horizon, had transformed the drab highway diner into a glowing sculpture. Big-eyed grasshoppers, their double wings clicking, skittered across the shimmering asphalt.

At dinner—four different food groups mixed together and covered with brown gravy—I attempted to make conversation with my mother.

"What do you suppose happened to Mr. Farley?" I asked.

In a low, disturbing tone of voice that I'd never heard my mother use before, she said, "If you don't mind, Andy, I'd rather not talk about that man—not now, not ever."

"Sure, Mom," I agreed, taken aback. "Whatever you say."

We continued our meal in silence while I considered the facts I'd gathered so far. Despite a growing number of suspects, I didn't feel that I was very close to solving this one. The only hard evidence I had was a missing person, plaid pajamas, and a pile of buttered popcorn—not much to go on.

I thought about the crimes I'd seen depicted on TV shows. In some of these mysteries, when a man suddenly goes missing—or worse—it turns out it has something to do with his wife. But Mr. Farley wasn't married. If the victim has no wife, suspicion often falls on his girlfriend. But Mr. Farley had no friends. If the victim has no wife and no girlfriend, then sometimes it turns out to be a jealous coworker who did it, someone who was after his job. But why would anybody want to be an assistant principal? It's the road to nowhere.

Perhaps it was a case of mistaken identity, I thought. *Whoever did it got the wrong guy.*

But in Mt. Mole, where everybody knows everybody — or at least, what their names are — it's not likely you'd get two people mixed up, except possibly the Fernelles, the town's only set of twins. But even when Doug Fernelle remembers to wear his toupee, he and Marianne aren't exactly what you'd call identical.

Looking up, I saw the stranger with the gray streak in his hair enter the restaurant.

What's he up to? I wondered.

My mother picked listlessly at her food, while across the room, the stranger slid into a booth and pulled a plastic-covered menu from a clip in the napkin holder. Suddenly, like band practice at Mt. Mole Middle School, the many sounds of the busy restaurant came together inside my head in one noisy, dissonant fanfare.

"I think I know what happened," I announced.

"What's that?" my mother responded.

"I think he was done in by a stranger," I said.

"Who?" she asked.

"Mr. Farley," I answered.

"Please, Andy," my mother snapped, pushing her plate away. "I meant what I said. I don't want to talk about — or even think about — that person."

For a fleeting, awkward moment, I wondered if my

31

mother, too, had some sort of grievance against Mr. Farley. Should her name be added to the suspect list? *What am I thinking?* I thought. *She's my mother!*

By the time we'd had our fill of the Knott Hungry's cuisine, night had fallen on the town of Mt. Mole. Although the wind had subsided, without the sun to heat the prairie earth, a chill was in the air. In the darkness, the distant, belly-shaped lump of Mt. Mole seemed larger than before. Could it be an optical illusion?

I gazed across the distance to the mountain's peak. In such flat surroundings, it was a dazzling sight. The lights coming from Knott Grande rivaled the twinkling of the stars.

"Have you ever been there?" I asked my mother.

"Where?" she replied.

"To the big house on the mountain," I answered. "To Knott Grande."

"Oh," she replied, again falling silent.

"Well, have you?" I insisted.

A faraway look appeared in my mother's eyes.

"Yes," she answered softly. "A long time ago."

"Really!" I exclaimed. "What was it like?"

My mother brushed a grasshopper from her shoulder and watched it bound away.

"Mt. Mole, the mountain, is a lot like Mt. Mole, the town," she replied. "Both are best seen from a distance."

A Town Meeting

Left to charge overnight, Pegasus — like me — is full of energy when morning comes. So more than an hour before the meeting about Mr. Farley was scheduled to begin, we were already at the cemetery, enjoying its peaceful, parklike setting on what promised to be a beautiful day.

In a scene straight from the panels of Big Laff Comics, shy rabbits peered around headstones, daffodils bounced like bobbleheads in the breeze, while butterflies, pale blue and flimsy as dust, jazz-danced over the graves of Mt. Moleans past. If it weren't for the fact that all its inhabitants were dead as doornails, you'd have sworn that Mt. Mole Memorial Gardens was a great place to live.

Eventually, an old car, in need of washing and riddled with rust, pulled into the cemetery entrance and chugged its way up the winding drive, sputtering to a stop at the chapel. I watched from a hundred yards away, expecting to see the lanky form of Reverend Oxide. Instead, a woman emerged, solidly constructed, and costumed in a loosely fitting purple dress. On her head, she wore a hat adorned with peacock feathers. In her right hand, she carried a shopping bag. When she turned her face in my direction and squinted in the bright sunlight, a sudden flash from her gold front tooth identified her as certainly as a message from a soldier's signal mirror. It was Mrs. Bagelbottom, my drama teacher.

"Andy!" she called in a loud, lilting voice, waving her arm in the air. "Are we the only ones here?"

With a nod of my head, I mimed a reply, then trotted to her car.

"Good morning," I said. "I see you came to honor Mr. Farley."

Mrs. Bagelbottom chuckled. "To tell the truth," she said, "I've never been a fan of Mr. Farley's. I'm only here because the Mt. Mole Chamber of Commerce asked me to give a dramatic reading. I suppose I'm the meeting's entertainment."

Mrs. Bagelbottom laughed again, this time so heartily that her whole body shook, a combination of sight and sound that set me to giggling, as well.

"So why didn't you like Mr. Farley?" I asked when I recovered.

"You mean apart from the fact that he was a jerk?" she replied.

"If you have other reasons," I said.

"Only that Mr. Farley was openly critical of my theater program," Mrs. Bagelbottom responded. "He said it was a waste of the students' time and the school's money."

"Ouch!" I exclaimed sympathetically.

"In his defense, I don't think he understood the arts," Mrs. Bagelbottom continued, shifting her shopping bag so she could scratch her nose. "Before he became an administrator, he taught earth sciences —you know, geology."

"Interesting," I said.

While we were talking, other people began arriving and entering the chapel.

"We'd better go inside," I suggested, taking Mrs. Bagelbottom's bag for her. "I wouldn't want to miss anything."

I seated my drama teacher near the front, then stepped away to study the room. Not surprisingly, I recognized just about everyone there—the *Chronicle* reporter, Mrs. Stitch, the chef from the restaurant, teachers from Mt. Mole Middle School. Chief Eagle Talon and his wife sat with members of the Mt. Mole Society for Railroad Preservation. The Fernelle twins were side by side in a middle pew. I also spotted Mr. Knott's personal assistant, the stranger with the gray streak in his hair, and the Wayne family from upstairs at the Knott Inn.

Boldly, I took a seat beside Georgia, realizing as I sat down that I was still clutching Mrs. Bagelbottom's shopping bag.

"Hello," I said cheerily. "Do you come here often?"

"Hardly ever," Georgia replied, the corners of her blue eyes crinkling as she smiled.

In front of us, a group of latecomers from Mt. Mole Martial Arts & Tanning took their seats.

"Looks like a pretty good turnout," I observed.

"What else do these people have to do with their time?" Georgia retorted.

Before I could come up with a response to her unexpected remark, Georgia had taken Mrs. Bagelbottom's shopping bag from my hand and opened it.

"Mmmm, popcorn!" she exclaimed. "Great idea!"

"What?" I said. "Let me see."

Sure enough, Mrs. Bagelbottom's bag contained the same starchy evidence that I'd been encountering ever since my investigation began.

"Oh, no," I moaned. "Not her, too!"

"Shhh!" Georgia hissed. "Father what's-his-name is speaking."

Reverend Oxide was standing with his arms extended.

"Shall we begin?" he asked.

"Okey-dokey," answered Doug Fernelle.

"We come together in unusual circumstances," Reverend Oxide intoned. "So often in this setting our hearts are heavy, but today, well . . ." The spiritual leader shrugged. "In any event, I invite you to look inside your hearts for something positive to contribute in Mr. Farley's memory. When you've found it, please share it with the rest of us."

The congregation sat in stone-faced silence, except for Georgia, who was noisily munching popcorn.

"Take your time," Reverend Farley advised. "Try to think of something you liked about the man."

36

Doug Fernelle, his toupee slightly askew, stood up.

"Ah," Reverend Oxide announced with relief. "Someone's thought of something."

"We're confused," Doug said. "Was this get-together called to figure out what happened to Farley, or is it his funeral?"

"Yeah," his sister, Marianne, added. "Why the bum's rush?"

Reverend Oxide's eyes flitted nervously around the room until they alighted on a tall, dark-haired man, Mr. Knott's personal assistant, Luis.

"Speaking for the Chamber of Commerce," Luis said, rising from his seat, "we feel that while what's happened may be unfortunate, what becomes of the town of Mt. Mole is of greater concern. So we propose taking this brief occasion to remember Mr. Farley, then moving on."

"Okey-dokey," Doug replied as he sat back down. "We were just wondering."

"I'm still wondering," complained his husky-voiced sister.

"Now," Reverend Oxide said, "does anybody have a pleasant anecdote concerning Mr. Farley?"

Again, the congregation fell into silence.

"You'd think they were all sixth-graders who forgot to do their homework," Georgia whispered in my ear.

"A kind word about Mr. Farley?" Reverend Oxide repeated. "Anyone?"

I began to feel embarrassed for Mr. Farley.

"This is terrible," I whispered to Georgia. "Even if he *was* disagreeable, somebody ought to say *something* nice about the man."

"How about you?" she said.

Never underestimate the power of a well-timed suggestion. It could be just the nudge someone needs. The next thing I knew, I was standing up and everybody in the chapel was looking at me.

"Andy," Reverend Oxide announced. "The floor is yours."

Fighting a surge of stage fright, I cleared my throat.

"I knew Mr. Farley," I improvised.

I paused to shuffle my feet and cough.

"Well, don't stop now," Georgia prodded.

"That is, I know him—sort of," I corrected myself. "As I see it, to Mr. Farley, speaking your mind truthfully is more important than protecting someone's feelings with well-meaning lies. With Mr. Farley, you always know exactly where you stand."

"That's why the rest of us are sitting down," muttered a railroad preservationist.

"Thank you, Andy," Reverend Oxide said, "for that food for thought."

"Speaking of food," the reporter for the *Weekly Mountain Chronicle* asked, "I was just wondering—are refreshments planned?"

"I'm featuring Chef's Surprise for lunch today,"

the chef from the Knott Hungry announced. "But get there early, because it'll go fast."

"You should try the daily double at my place," Mrs. Stitch suggested. "Even if you don't have a dog, it's the best deal in town."

"I brought popcorn," Mrs. Bagelbottom said, "but I can't remember where I put it."

"Thank you, folks," Reverend Oxide called out, tapping for attention. "To continue with the program, Mrs. Cynthia Bagelbottom will read from her new play about Mt. Mole's legendary Spanish forebear, Francisco Vásquez de Coronado. It's called *Montaña del Oro — The Mountain of Gold*."

Like a thunderstorm rolling across the prairie, my drama teacher swept to the center of the room and, in the commanding tones of a seasoned stage performer, began to speak.

"My first thought was, he lied in every word . . ." she began.

"This meeting is an insult to Mr. Farley," I whispered to Georgia. "I'll bet if he were here right now, he'd get up and leave."

"The fact that nobody's doing that should tell you something," Georgia replied.

"What do you mean?" I asked.

"That as bad as it is, it's still the best entertainment in town," she said.

For the next half hour, Mrs. Bagelbottom performed excerpts from her play. As fond as I was of her, however, I found her presentation disappointing, in part because it included such unsettling images as "one stiff, blind horse, his every bone a-stare," "toads in a poisoned tank," and "wild cats in a red-hot iron cage," and also because it had nothing to do with Mr. Farley. Indeed, not another word was spoken about the missing assistant principal until after the town meeting had adjourned.

I was just stepping onto Pegasus when the stranger with the gray streak in his hair approached.

"I enjoyed your remarks in there," he said.

"Thank you," I replied.

"Did Mr. Farley have any other friends?" he asked. "Or were you the only one?"

I must have let my mouth fall open, so great was my astonishment at being called Mr. Farley's friend. How else could that grasshopper have flown in?

The Kindness of Strangers

He introduced himself as Dr. Whitney Blemish, the state's psychologist-at-large.

"The governor sent me," he explained. "I'm here to lend a helping hand to the citizens of Mt. Mole."

"Great!" I said, spitting out the bitter taste of grasshopper juice. "So you think you can help us find Mr. Farley?"

"Actually," Dr. Blemish explained, as the last few

stragglers made their way to the parking lot, "my skills are more in the direction of helping people get in touch with their feelings."

"Oh," I replied, waving to Chief Eagle Talon and his wife as they walked by. "I see."

"Your town's had a few setbacks lately," Dr. Blemish observed. "Some people might find the circumstances discouraging."

But the psychologist's words were cut short by Mrs. Bagelbottom.

"Excuse me," she interjected. "I don't mean to intrude, but I was so impressed by Andy's contribution to the meeting that I simply had to ask: Andy, will you be in my play?"

"I guess so," I agreed. "If you want me to."

"How wonderful!" Mrs. Bagelbottom exclaimed.

With much rustling and fluttering, she continued to her car. But before I could pick up where I left off with Dr. Blemish, one of the Fernelle twins tapped me on the arm.

"Hey, Andy," Marianne Fernelle interrupted, her raspy voice suggesting someone getting over a cold. "Is your mother working today? My locks are losing their bounce."

"She should be there now," I answered.

"That's a relief," Marianne said, sauntering away with her brother.

"You seem to get along well with everybody," Dr. Blemish observed.

"Oh, I don't know," I said modestly. "It's just because Mt. Mole is more like a family than a town."

"Perhaps," Dr. Blemish replied, running his fingers through his hair. "But it's a family with plenty of family secrets."

I nodded my head as if I understood.

"Well, I'd better be going," Dr. Blemish announced, glancing at his wristwatch. "Can you direct me to Butcher Beauty College?"

"That's easy," I said. "It's where my mother works —eighteen blocks that way, at Third and Butterfly. Just follow the Fernelles."

Thanking me, he got into a gray station wagon bearing an official state seal.

He must be who he says he is, I thought.

I watched as the station wagon crossed the highway, caught up with a pickup truck, and headed into the business district. In the far distance, the lump-shaped mountain loomed malevolently in the noonday sun. Somehow, it seemed larger.

"Is this your scooter," a voice behind me asked.

I turned to face the sparkling blue eyes of Georgia Wayne.

"Hey," I greeted her, my heart leaping up. "Long time, no see."

"This is such a cool machine," Georgia said. "Mind if I take it for a spin?"

She placed her hand on the upright to the handle-bar, her slender fingers wrapping around the black steel tube like a professional ballplayer confidently picking up a bat.

"Sorry," I replied, with a self-conscious laugh. "Nobody drives Pegasus but me. It's a personal rule. But we'd be glad to give you a lift home."

For a fraction of a second, a pout flickered across Georgia's face, but as quickly as it appeared, it transformed itself into a classic cover-girl smile.

"Okay!" Georgia agreed. "Where do I sit?"

"You stand up," I explained. "Get behind me and hold on tight."

Once you've crossed the highway, it's only four blocks to the Knott Blue Ribbon Inn, a journey that lasts little longer than a carnival ride. So to prolong my good fortune, instead of turning right at Fifth from Squirrel Street, I veered left, away from the Knott Inn. The sudden turn caused my pretty passenger to grip me tighter, for which I silently congratulated myself.

"Does the mountain look any different to you today?" I asked.

"It the same ugly pimple that it's always been," Georgia answered, raising her voice over the high-pitched hum of the scooter. "Why? Were you expecting it to become beautiful?"

"I think it's gotten bigger," I replied. "It's as if the mountain were expanding."

"Maybe it just seems that way because the town is getting smaller," Georgia suggested.

"People *are* leaving Mt. Mole," I admitted. "Especially since the tornado."

"Can you blame them?" Georgia asked. "What's to keep anybody here? My father says if he could only find enough pieces of our house, he'd sell it. He can't stand this place!"

"He can't?" I repeated, taking a right at Raccoon. "But he's hardly given us a chance."

A feeling like the first sign of a serious illness welled up inside me.

Surely, Georgia won't move away, I thought.

"My father thinks the town's problems go pretty deep," Georgia added. "He says Mt. Mole is rotten to the core."

Curiously, as she spoke these words, a faint but bitter aroma wafted through the air, a hard-to-place, disconcerting smell, like a far-off chemical spill or someone's plastic-wrapped dinner burning in the microwave oven.

"Maybe so," I said, sniffing the air like a hound on the hunt, "but that's not a good enough reason to give up on your home."

"It's not *my* home," Georgia muttered.

Rather than have an argument, I let the matter drop, concentrating instead on the unbroken pace of Pegasus and the unplanned proximity of Georgia. At Seventh Street, I turned right again, doubling back toward the motel, pouring on the power with the handlebar-mounted calipers until, to my dismay,

Pegasus suddenly grew silent and glided to a stop.

"What's wrong?" Georgia asked.

"Out of juice," I replied. "Battery needs a recharge. Do you think you can walk from here?"

Georgia laughed. Pegasus had quit just half a block from the entrance to the Knott Inn. Next door, at the restaurant, cars were filling the parking lot.

"Looks like we're in time for lunch," she said. "Why don't we wash up, then meet in the lobby, okay?"

"Sure," I agreed.

Once in my room, I plugged Pegasus into the wall to recharge, washed my hands, and ran a comb through my unruly hair. When I looked into the mirror above the sink, I wasn't happy with what I saw, and I don't mean my slightly soiled, windblown clothes. What I found discouraging was my face — my eyes, my nose, and, most of all, my mouth, the way it turned down at one side as if I were all set to frown.

But what could I do about it?

My face isn't who I am, I thought. *It's no more the real me than a costume from one of Mrs. Bagelbottom's plays!*

But did Georgia Wayne know this? I wondered. Did she have any idea who lived inside this borrowed shell?

Turning sideways, I faced another mirror, a full-length one, attached with screws to the bathroom door. From this position, I could see the mirror above the sink over my shoulder, one mirror reflected in the other, a mirror within a mirror within a mirror, creating a row of identical Andys as far as the eye could see.

People see only the first Andy, I thought. *But there are all those other Andys hidden underneath.*

As had happened before, this kind of dreamy, introspective thinking promptly summoned forth its own brand of punishment. On turning to leave the bathroom, I slipped on a thin, wet sliver of motel soap stuck to the slick tile floor. In an instant, I found myself lying on my back, staring into swirling galaxies of stars.

No more philosophizing! I said quietly to myself. *I promise!*

A Sign of Trouble

"Sorry," Georgia apologized, slurping a soupy spoonful of navy beans with sliced hot dogs, "but when you didn't show up in the lobby, I figured you'd changed your mind."

"It almost got changed permanently," I replied, rubbing my head. "Is that the Chef's Surprise?"

"Mmm-hmm," Georgia confirmed. "Want some?"

"Not really," I said.

With a charm that you had to be there to

appreciate, Georgia pursed her lips and dabbed delicately at her face with a paper napkin, blotting sauce first from one corner of her mouth, then the other, a ritual she repeated several times. For some reason, I found her movements fascinating—like watching a raccoon washing fruit in a mountain stream. But the mind, it seems, is weightless. It drifts from thought to thought. The sight of Georgia's paper napkin on her lips reminded me of the list of suspects that I'd started, and my attention shifted from the table manners of the prettiest girl in town to the plight of Mt. Mole's most unpopular man.

"Tell me something," I said. "If you wanted to get rid of somebody, how would you go about doing it?"

"I'd ask them to leave," Georgia replied.

"What if they refused?" I asked. "And they did it in such a way that you were insulted."

"I guess I'd get mad," Georgia answered.

The harried waitress rushed by, and with a clatter and a thump deposited a plateful of beanie-weenies in front of me. I pushed the offering across the table to Georgia, who promptly returned her napkin to her lap and tackled the steaming dish with gusto. Each time she took a bite, she closed her eyes, savoring the sensation.

"How mad?" I persisted.

"I don't know," she said. "If they kept bugging me, I might get angry enough to slug them."

"So there's a point at which you'd resort to

violence," I summarized, noting how the shaft of sunlight through the window caused the blonde hairs on Georgia's forearm to glow like tiny neon lights.

"I guess so," she said. "Are you going to eat your roll?"

"You can have it," I replied.

"Why all the questions?" she asked.

"I think that's what happened to Mr. Farley," I answered. "I think he made somebody so mad that they decided to shut him up for good."

"Why are you wasting your time worrying about that guy?" Georgia asked, soaking my dinner roll in beanie-weenie sauce. "He was so crabby all the time."

In my mind, I could see myself standing in front of the bathroom mirror, where identical Andys, like cloned soldiers on parade, duplicated themselves into infinity. Suddenly, the images morphed into endless copies of an older, taller person — a scowling man wearing thick, black-rimmed glasses.

"Hello?" Georgia called, waving her hand in my face. "Anybody seen Andy?"

"What?" I responded, the mental image of multiple Mr. Farleys popping like soap bubbles in a spring breeze.

"I asked you why you're wasting your time with someone who was so mean to everybody," Georgia repeated.

"He wasn't mean to me," I replied.

Georgia put down her spoon. "Well, I'll be," she said. "So you *were* a friend of Mr. Farley's."

Before I could react, the glowing filaments on Georgia's forearm disappeared in a dark and ominous shadow. I turned around to see the front window of the Lucius Knott Hungry Family Restaurant being covered up from outside.

"What's going on?" I asked.

"Beats me," Georgia replied. "Maybe we should take a look."

Seconds later, we were out on the sidewalk staring at a pair of red-and-blue signs, one attached to the Knott Hungry's window, the other fluttering from the canvas canopy of the Knott Blue Ribbon Inn next door. Their wording was identical.

FOR SALE. PRIME COMMERCIAL PROPERTY. CONTACT KNOTT REAL ESTATE ASSOCIATES, MT. MOLE.

"Mr. Knott is selling out?" I said, surprised. "Why would he want to do that?"

From out on the prairie, from the rounded mound of Mt. Mole, came a low, faint, rumbling sound—a sound more felt than heard, like overloaded trucks passing on some busy, distant highway. No sooner had the vibration subsided than a thin plume of gray-white smoke rose like Marley's ghost over Knott Grande. Closer at hand, from the parched front lawn of the Knott Hungry Family Restaurant, startled grasshoppers swarmed into the air, their wings

49

clacking like plastic spoons, while on the sidewalk, the bent-legged Vesuvius broke free from the leash in Miss Futon's hand, spun around in circles, and howled like a coyote.

"Good grief!" I exclaimed. "What on earth was that?"

"I'm sure I don't know," Georgia replied. "But whatever it was, it can't be good."

Lost and Found

Something told me time was running out for Mr. Farley. But so far, all my feeble efforts to find him had been in vain. If I were a character in a comic book, this would be the panel where you'd see my conscience sneaking up behind me, delivering a swift kick to my rear end.

Heck, I thought. *I'm not an investigator, I'm a procrastinator. It's high time I went out and found something!*

"I think I'll take a walk to work off that lunch," I announced, patting my stomach and grimacing. "I'll see you later,"

"But you didn't eat anything," Georgia protested.

"It won't be a long walk," I replied.

While Pegasus continued to recharge in my room, and with no plan other than high hopes and an open mind, I headed south on Toad, letting my feet set a leisurely pace in order not to miss anything worth detecting.

The sun was warm. The air was clear. A light breeze was blowing in my face. In the branches overhead, new leaves fluttered like minnows mingling at the edge of a pond. Throughout the town of Mt. Mole, the after-lunch lull was settling in.

Nothing out of the ordinary here, I thought.

At Ninth Street, my feet automatically turned east toward Muskrat. For a brief moment, I thought I heard the sound of footsteps behind me, but when I turned and squinted into the distance, all I could see were black dots moving in the grass.

Do I need glasses? I wondered.

I concluded that what I was looking at were robins, those placid, poker-faced inspectors of Mt. Mole's lawns and gardens. Just ahead, such a bird was perched imperiously atop a Knott Real Estate For Sale sign, one of dozens of red-and-blue signs of surrender that had materialized overnight like mushrooms after a hard rain.

Honestly, I thought, *if you didn't know better, you'd think the whole town was for sale.*

Crossing Porcupine, I could hear the erratic lurching of construction equipment up ahead, as again I sensed the movement of someone behind me. Pausing, I bent over, pretending to tie my shoelaces, while stealing a glance down the sidewalk.

At a house near Quail, I thought I saw someone

crouching behind a privet hedge, but after rubbing my eyes, I concluded it was only a rabbit.

Just past Opossum, I entered the restricted area, where Mt. Mole's only bulldozer was struggling to move debris left in the roadway by the tornado — piles of worthless rubble that once had been important stuff in people's lives.

My feet, it seemed, left to their own devices, had carried me straight home, not to my makeshift residence at Mr. Knott's motel, but to the corner of Ninth Street and Muskrat, where my house once stood. Now, of course, there were only remains — a basement, a front porch, concrete steps, and some miscellaneous structural parts half-buried in the dirt like bones. Although it was a sight I'd seen several times before, it still packed a wallop.

With a heaviness in my heart, I collapsed on the curb, displacing a sleeping grasshopper that spiraled into the air and landed like a circus acrobat in the middle of the street.

I don't know how long I sat there, but it must have been quite a while. I remember thinking about how some people, spared by the tornado, found other people's possessions intact inside their houses.

There was one report of a complete set of dinner dishes discovered in a neighbor's kitchen cabinet, and another of a family's clean, folded laundry stacked six blocks away on an old woman's bed. It was as if poltergeists had been at work in Mt. Mole. For days afterward, conversation centered on why certain homes were destroyed while others managed to escape nature's wrath.

I recall Mr. Farley's comment afterward. "There are only two possible explanations," he'd said in the hallway at school. "Either this town is so awful it had it coming, or life isn't fair." I'm guessing that he meant people don't always deserve what happens to them.

The ruins that lay before me now had been the only home I'd ever known. I thought of what I missed most about it, not the things my mother had given me over the years, but the good times, now lost, sucked up by dark, deadly clouds and spit out in some faraway, unfathomable place.

Although it turned out to be one of unprecedented significance, try as I might, I could recall nothing noteworthy about the day preceding the tornado. It must have been a perfectly ordinary day.

How could I have known? How can *anybody* know when a day is destined to be the last of its kind?

And what would we do differently if we could?

Had Mr. Farley's last day been unremarkable as well? I wondered.

He'd been watching people making speeches about something called vulcanology. Vulcanology! Of all the things in the world there are to think about!

My nose brought me to my senses. Smelling what

my brain at first thought were flowers, the subtle aromatic signal steadily increased until at last I determined that it was shampoo, the kind provided in little bottles by the Lucius Knott Blue Ribbon Inn.

It took only a millisecond to put two and two together.

"You followed me," I announced matter-of-factly.

"Just expressing my heartfelt curiosity," Georgia Wayne replied, stepping from behind the tangled roots of an upended hickory tree. "What's going on?"

"I was hoping to find a clue about Mr. Farley," I explained. "Something brought me here."

"I see," Georgia said, staring into the hole that once had been my house. "So where was your room?"

I pointed into the air. "Upstairs," I answered. "On the second floor, at the front."

Georgia put a hand above her eyes and gazed into the distance.

"Looks like you might have had a view of Mt. Mole," she said.

"I could see Knott Grande above the rooftops," I confirmed.

"Not so many rooftops, now," she pointed out, looking to the north across the splintered houses, one of which, a few streets over, had briefly been her own. "Makes that dirt pile out there easier to find."

"Yes," I agreed. "Especially now that it's gotten bigger."

"You've got Mt. Mole on the brain," Georgia scoffed, tossing her gold hair in the sun. "I'm worried about you."

"Something about that mountain isn't right," I insisted.

"Isn't that the truth!" Georgia exclaimed. "How about the fact that people around here insist on calling it a mountain! Holy Toledo, Andy, it's only — what? — a hundred and sixty-five feet high? Did you know that Mt. Everest is over twenty-nine thousand feet above sea level? Now, that's a mountain! And Everest is so hard to climb that it's claimed the lives of nearly two hundred climbers! What's it take to conquer Mt. Mole? A stroll on a Sunday afternoon?"

"That's where you're wrong, Georgia," I said. "Nobody goes to the top of Mt. Mole except Mr. Knott and the people who work for him."

"Whatever," Georgia responded, her blue eyes wandering over the tornado-flattened scene. "You know," she mused, "if you hadn't led me here, I would never have been able to find your house. This part of town is little more than an empty grid — just crisscrossed streets with a few fallen trees and lots of gaping basements. It's impossible to tell which street is which."

"I've memorized the route," I said.

"Even the dirt around here has changed," Georgia observed.

Looking down, I could see that she was right. No longer black like the rich prairie earth it once had been, the soil where my house had stood was now lighter and grittier, with flecks of shiny particles mixed in — man-made materials pulverized and deposited by the tornado. Absent-mindedly, I picked up a stick and scrawled Georgia's name in the dust.

"Is that your list of suspects?" she asked with a grin.

Embarrassed, I erased my handiwork. "That's the problem," I explained. "There are too many of them — so many it makes my brain spin. I hardly know where to begin."

"It's usually the one you least suspect," she stated confidently.

"If that were true," I replied, "then the one you least suspect would become the one you most suspect, which would automatically make somebody else the one you least suspect, ruling out the first person altogether."

"Huh?" Georgia asked.

Undaunted, I continued. "Then the new least-suspected person would move up to become the most-suspected, which then would rule that person out, only to be followed by the next person from the bottom of the list, and the next, and the next, and so on. Eventually this would include everybody, which is the very problem that I started out with. No offense, Georgia, but your theory solves nothing."

Georgia shook her head and sighed.

"I think you're trying too hard," she suggested. "Maybe instead of looking for the solution, you should just relax and let the solution come to you."

"That's what Chief Eagle Talon does," I replied. "But I don't put much faith in that technique. It seems too much like magic."

"Have you ever done it?" she asked.

"Not exactly," I answered. "What would be the point?"

"The point," Georgia said, placing her hand over my eyes, "is to let your mind do the walking. Now settle back and think of anything but Mr. Farley."

This, of course, is much easier said than done. If someone advises you not to think of vampires, for example, flapping capes and dripping fangs will be the first things to spring to mind. Similarly, when the doctor says, "Now don't think about it, and this won't hurt a bit," you can be sure that the pain that follows will be excruciating. But such was the combined power of Georgia's soft-spoken suggestion and gentle touch that in no time at all I'd cleared my mind of all things Farley and drifted off to thoughts from long ago—a neighbor's kittens, the fifth grade dance, my first time alone at the movies.

The experience was one that's impossible to describe, so take my word for it when I say that it was better than an afternoon nap, and better, too, than dreaming. How long I remained in this blissful, semihypnotic state I don't know, but the force that had launched my mental journey was the same one that abruptly brought me back.

"Good golly!" Georgia exclaimed. "The popcorn's moving!"

"What?" I said, shaking my head vigorously from side to side in an effort to restart my brain. "What popcorn?"

"Right there!" she cried. "By your foot."

Where Georgia was pointing, I could see only sparkling rocks and dried mud, but as my eyes took on the task of sorting through the many shades of dark and light, I spied one small, popcorn-sized rock climbing clumsily over a clod of dirt.

"Stony!" I cried.

Miraculously, my long-lost pet was still alive!

"You know this thing?" Georgia asked.

"You bet I do," I answered, scooping up the little crustacean into the palm of my hand. In his excitement, Stony tickled me with his tiny legs, trans- mitting a smile from my fingertips to my face. "He's my hermit crab. He's been missing for weeks."

"Hmmm," Georgia murmured dubiously.

"You don't know how much this means to me," I explained. "I'm so happy, I could kiss you."

Underneath the strands of blonde hair that spilled down her forehead, Georgia's blue eyes darted to and fro, as if weighing the pros and cons of my suggestion.

"That's okay," she replied. "Why don't you just kiss your little lobster, instead. I'm sure he's missed you."

Teacher's Pet

Thanking me for the most interesting day she'd had in Mt. Mole since the day her house blew away, Georgia Wayne patted my hand, squeezed my shoulder, and left Stony and me standing in the doorway of my room at the Knott Inn.

Naturally, I was happy to be reunited with my pet. Using the plastic ice bucket provided for the room, I fashioned a terrarium for him, placing it in a safe, out-of-the-way corner of the combination chest of drawers, desk, and TV stand.

After so many frightening days, lost and alone in the great outdoors, the diminutive beach creature seemed pleased with his manageable surroundings. Methodically, he explored his habitat, inspecting every pebble, puddle, and hiding place. I marveled at how focused he seemed to be. Stony was a creature who left no grain of sand unturned.

Unlike me.

It's not that I'm lazy, I thought. *It's just too easy to become distracted.*

Could this be a character flaw? If so, it's no wonder I'd made such little progress in finding Assistant Principal Farley. I was struggling to overcome a trait I was born with.

But where did I get my genes?

Half came from my mother, a hard-working person whom I'd known for years. But what about the other half of my genetic makeup? What did I know about my father?

Nothing. Nothing at all.

No matter how much I pressed her, my mother remained steadfastly silent on that subject. For all I knew about him, my father may as well have been the mist on the mountain.

Sighing, I watched my hard-working hermit crab assemble a shelter from a pair of yellowed philodendron leaves. It occurred to me that while Stony's reappearance had been a nice surprise — something of a miracle, actually, or at the very least a comic book–style coincidence — it wasn't likely that Mr. Farley would show up in the same convenient way. Despite what Georgia suggested and Chief Eagle Talon believed, in my experience, the solutions to life's nagging problems rarely arrive like postcards in the mail. Most require effort.

Go to the hermit crab, you sluggard, I advised myself. *Consider its ways and be wise.*

Successful detective work is slow, steady, and hermit crab–like. It's a careful gathering, evaluating, and piecing together of clues. I'd started out okay, considering various hypotheses, visiting the crime scene, conducting interviews with a few of the people whom Mr. Farley had rubbed the wrong way: Mrs. Stitch, Earl, Reverend Oxide. But what was I overlooking?

What about Mr. Farley's friends? I thought. Surely there was someone in Mt. Mole that he got along with. Even the Grinch who stole Christmas had a friend. Of course, it was his dog.

Suddenly, I was struck by one of those insights that in comic books is signaled by a light bulb going *BING!* above an astonished character's head.

Dog? I thought. *Vesuvius!*

The light bulb over my head faded and in its place the face of Miss Futon appeared.

"Poor, poor Jacob," she was saying. "He's gone! Vanished!"

Of course! I thought. *I never knew his first name. Could Jacob be Mr. Farley?*

Instead of interviewing all the people in town who disliked Mr. Farley—a group that no doubt numbered in the hundreds—maybe I should talk to someone who cared enough about him to feel sorry he was no longer around.

I looked at the clock. There was just enough time before dinner.

Unplugging Pegasus, I rolled the scooter out the door and into the motel parking lot, setting off at a pleasant fifteen miles per hour. Within a couple of minutes, I'd traced a route one block south and ten blocks east, to Seventh and Jackalope, on the other side of the storm swath, where I coasted to a stop in front of a modest yellow bungalow.

Miss Futon's house was ablaze with flowers. Daffodils, tulips, and crocuses sprang from freshly mulched gardens that hugged the foundation of my English teacher's home like a bright feather boa on an actress's neck. Clown-faced pansies burst from window boxes, pots, and planters on a wide, covered porch. But in contrast to this all this cultivated beauty was a dry front lawn teeming with grasshoppers — fat, brown, and menacing — a swirling, clacking sea of insects, and every one of them seemed hopping mad. Miss Futon's house, and perhaps all of Mt. Mole, was under attack. Cautiously, I remained on the sidewalk.

I could wait until nightfall, I thought. *Or I could risk it.*

At that moment, the front door opened and Miss Futon's elderly dog, Vesuvius, emerged, moving like a spider down the stairs, one stiff, creaky leg at a time. With agonizing effort, the ancient canine reached the front yard. After much circling and sniffing, he located a well-browned patch of grass, squatted like a plastic Cootie toy, and began to pee.

Well, I thought. *She must be home.*

Tentatively, I stepped toward the house. Immediately, streams of goggle-eyed grasshoppers rose up and flitted through the air, as if spit from an automatic sprinkler system. Common sense forced me to retreat to the sidewalk. Throughout this assault, however, Miss Futon's dog continued his endless squirting.

"Andy?" a voice called out. "What are you doing here?"

Armed with a long-handled insecticide pump, Miss Futon had rounded the corner enveloped in a thick — and deadly — chemical cloud.

"Oh, hello," I replied cheerfully. "I was just passing by."

Wearing a floppy hat, sunglasses, and denim overalls cut like shorts, my English teacher might have been a fashion model enjoying a day off, except she didn't seem particularly happy. When Miss Futon approached, I could see that she wasn't wearing sunglasses to protect her eyes from glare, but to hide her puffy, tear-stained face.

Uh, oh, I thought. *Either she's gotten a whiff of her bug spray or she's been crying again.*

"I may have come at a bad time," I said politely.

As if to illustrate the power of my suggestion, the elderly, patchy-haired dog, concluding his contribution to the spotted lawn, suddenly gasped, rolled his eyes, and keeled over, giving up all claims to consciousness as abruptly and effortlessly as a sneeze.

"Vesuvius!" Miss Futon cried, rushing to the

motionless dog's side. "Vesuvius, bark to me!"

But Vesuvius was down for the count. Only the gentle rise and fall of his fat, pink, liver-spotted belly hinted that he might still be alive.

"Boo-hoo-hoo," Miss Futon wailed, cradling the dormant dog in her arms. "Boo-hoo-hoo-hoo-hoo!"

As the tears tumbled down Miss Futon's face, soaking the bib of her overalls, I found myself torn between a desire to lend comfort and a trouble-sniffing instinct that urged, *Quick! Run away!*

What, I wondered, *do I do now?*

With a sigh of resignation, I yielded to my better self. Slapping grasshoppers away from my face, I dashed to my anguished English teacher's kneeling form and gently placed my hand on her shoulder.

"I'll help you carry him into the house," I said.

Later, with Vesuvius snoring peacefully on his bed, I sat with Miss Futon in her parlor, sipping tea.

"He's done that before," she informed me. "It must be getting close to his time."

"Maybe it's the bug spray," I suggested. "If it can kill grasshoppers, it's bound to be bad for dogs. How old is he, anyway?"

"Vesuvius is seventeen," she replied.

I did some quick calculations in my head.

"Holy smokes!" I exclaimed. "That's a hundred and nineteen dog years!"

Miss Futon nodded and sipped her tea.

"I know," she said. "But I'm hoping he can last a little longer. I can't imagine losing both of them in the same week."

"Both of them?" I repeated.

"Vesuvius," she explained, her lower lip trembling as she stifled a sniffle, "and Jacob. It's as if my whole world were blowing up."

Ironically, just as Miss Futon spoke the words "blowing up," a low, deep sound like muffled thunder came from somewhere out on the prairie. It was the same strange reverberation I'd heard with Georgia.

"There it goes again!" I exclaimed, spilling tea onto Miss Futon's plush carpet. "It's like someone's blasting rock at the mountain."

"Oh, dear!" Miss Futon cried. "This isn't good."

"No," I agreed, "it surely isn't. But just to clarify, are you referring to your carpet, the explosion, or the recent disappearance of Mr. Farley?"

With the suddenness of a blast ripping through the surface of the earth, Miss Futon's pent-up grief burst through her mind's defenses.

"Boo-hoo-hoo!" she wailed. "Boo-hoo-hoo-hoo-hoo!"

Such was the force of my teacher's caterwauling that my teacup, half-emptied by the jolt of the first unexpected sound, now completed the job in my lap.

Dang! I thought, jumping up from my chair.

Clearly, wherever the state's traveling psychologist was at the moment, he wasn't where he was needed most.

"Maybe I'd better be getting home," I suggested.

"Please stay, Andy," Miss Futon whimpered, dabbing her eyes with a tissue and handing the box to me. "There's something about Jacob and me that you need to know."

Uh, oh, I thought. *I'm not sure I'm ready for this.*

Miss Futon paused to blow her nose.

"More tea?" she asked. "Something to eat? How about some popcorn? It only takes a minute in the microwave."

Blotting my trousers, I backed toward the door.

"Listen," I said, my hand on the doorknob. "If you're about to confess that Mr. Farley's body is buried out there underneath your flowers, maybe I should go get Chief Eagle Talon."

"Don't be ridiculous, Andy," Miss Futon said. "What I was going to say is that Jacob and I have recently been engaged—"

"So that's it!" I exclaimed, smacking my fist into my palm. "It's a love story! Why, that explains everything!"

As I leapt gleefully around the room, Miss Futon's face changed from sad to slightly amused, as if she were watching a performance of one of Mrs. Bagelbottom's middle school comedies.

"Please, Andy," Miss Futon insisted. "Let me

finish. This is hard enough as it is."

Smirking from the satisfaction of putting two and two together, I flopped into my chair and gazed at my English teacher in a whole new light. No doubt Mr. Farley had been attracted by her simple beauty. But what, I wondered, had she seen in him?

"What I'm trying to tell you, Andy," she said, "is that Jacob and I have been engaged in independent scientific research."

She folded her hands in her lap. Curiously, I could see no engagement ring on Miss Futon's finger. Perhaps Mr. Farley, being an underpaid public educator, couldn't afford one, I concluded.

"He's been looking into seismic abnormalities in the Mt. Mole region," she continued. "I've been editing his notes for a paper he was to present at the International Conference on Vulcanology in Honolulu in June."

"I see," I responded, hearing little and understanding less, except the part about Honolulu. "So after a June wedding, you're planning to honeymoon in Hawaii?"

"Wedding? Honeymoon?" Miss Futon repeated, startled. "Who said anything about getting married?"

"You said you were engaged," I explained. "Engagements don't last forever. Eventually, you tie the knot."

Miss Futon's face twisted into a scowl. "Andy,"

she said, "do you know why you continue to get B's when you're perfectly capable of making A's? I'll tell you why. It's because you don't pay attention."

"Excuse me?" I responded. "Could you repeat that?"

Miss Futon shot me a look of extreme annoyance. "Listen closely," she ordered. "Jacob Farley and I have been conducting scientific research. We are not —repeat *not*—getting married. Why, I could never be interested in a man like that. Except for occasional, inadvertent acts of kindness, which are few and far between, he's just what everybody says he is—a rude, uncaring hothead."

"So you're saying he *is* buried in your garden?" I summarized.

Miss Futon's exasperation with me had reached a breaking point. Storming over to where I stood, she yanked open the door and shook her forefinger in my face.

"Now, get this straight, Andy Forrest," she fumed. "Jacob Farley is a business associate, that's all. He was paying me to help him with a paper. It would make no sense for me to wish him dead."

On the word "dead," Miss Futon erupted into a long sequence of sobs that shook her slender body from stem to stern.

"Boo-hoo-hoo!" she wailed. "Boo-hoo-hoo-hoo-hoo!"

Well, I wondered. *Does she like Mr. Farley?*

When the earth was formed out of solar flares and stardust, it must have been a very difficult place to understand, I figured. But putting people on it—especially people as different as men and women—has only made matters worse.

Perhaps I'll never know, I concluded.

Naturally, such amateur philosophizing came at a price. No sooner did this accidental, idle thought pass through my brain than a trembling in the earth shook Miss Futon's house, causing the door to slam shut on my hand.

"Yi-yi-yi!" I hollered.

"Boo-hoo-hoo!" Miss Futon chimed in. "Boo-hoo-hoo-hoo-hoo!"

The Nose on Your Face

That evening at the Knott Hungry, few people bothered to complain about the food. They were much too busy talking about the peculiar vibrations coming from the mountain.

"I'll bet it's a secret, underground weapons test," one of the Fernelle twins speculated. "The government's behind it—just you wait and see."

"If you ask me," the other Fernelle croaked, "I'd say old man Knott's discovered oil on his property and is drilling himself a well."

"That's always the way," a railroad preservationist

joined in. "The rich keep getting richer, while the rest of us—well, let me put it this way—have you tasted this fish?"

"A For Sale sign went up on the bank today," my mother announced.

I pushed my plate of boiled fish and rice aside.

"The Knott Secure Savings and Loan is for sale?" I said. "Is our money okay?"

"I certainly hope so," my mother answered.

"I wonder—" I began, stopping myself in mid-question.

"Wonder what?" my mother asked.

"Never mind," I replied. "You'll think it's too far-fetched."

"Try me," she persisted.

"Well," I complied, "what if everything is connected? What if the noises coming from the mountain, the signs popping up all over town, and the disappearance of that person whose name shall not be mentioned are pieces of some much bigger picture?"

My mother glared at me.

"I can't imagine how," she said.

"Is this chair taken?" a man's voice asked.

Grateful for the interruption, we looked up to see Dr. Blemish standing beside our table, a gift-wrapped package tucked beneath his arm.

"Oh!" my mother said, jumping in her seat and pushing her hair away from her face. "Please join us."

Dr. Blemish seated himself between my mother and me.

"Have you completed your interviews?" my mother asked.

"I've talked to a number of people," Dr. Blemish answered. "But I'm having trouble seeing Mr. Knott."

"That doesn't surprise me," my mother said.

"No?" Dr. Blemish responded.

"Mr. Knott isn't fond of outsiders," she explained.

"Hmmm," Dr. Blemish replied. "Not exactly what I'd expect to find in a Chamber of Commerce president."

"Is *anything* about Mt. Mole what you expected?" my mother asked.

Dr. Blemish laughed, his eyes fixed on my mother's face, as the waitress placed a plate in front of him.

"Do your travels take you all over?" I interjected, in an effort to be included in the conversation.

"I've been to every nook and cranny in the state," Dr. Blemish replied, "except for Mt. Mole. This is my first visit." He leaned toward my mother and added softly, "But now that I'm here, I can see I've saved the best for last."

"Is the whole state as flat as this?" I inquired.

"It's even flatter," the psychologist explained. "Thanks to that curious anomaly you call a mountain. There's nothing quite like it anywhere else."

"I've been thinking about that mountain," I said,

71

"and a few other things, besides, and one thing I was wondering is—"

"He's had a lot on his mind, lately," my mother interrupted. "How's your dinner?"

"Interesting flavor," Dr. Blemish answered.

My mother's behavior took me aback. Had I embarrassed her? Or was this an attempt to keep me from bringing up the subject of Mr. Farley? Resolutely, I pressed on.

"What I was wondering is, hasn't anybody ever questioned why Mt. Mole exists?" I asked. "Surely I can't be the only person who's wondered how there can be this great big mound in a place that's flatter than Chief Eagle Talon's feet. What is it? How did it get there? And why is there only the one? Don't mountains usually come in groups?"

"Hmmm," Dr. Blemish replied, running his fingers through the streak in his hair, as if trying to stimulate his brain to come up with the answer. "Perhaps you should pose that question to a geologist."

"Roll?" my mother asked, passing the bread bowl to Dr. Blemish, who, like the rest of us, had abandoned the fish.

"Why, thank you," Dr. Blemish replied, hesitating before adding, "Irene."

"My pleasure," my mother said, to which, after brief consideration, she appended, "Whitney."

I coughed into my napkin to get their attention.

"The only geologist in Mt. Mole that I know of,"

I announced, defiantly continuing the conversation from the point at which my mother had forced it off the road, "is a man I didn't find out was a geologist until it was too late to ask him anything at all—the missing Mr. Farley. Unfortunately, nobody seems to be interested in finding him but me."

My mother shot me a look that could have stopped a rat at forty paces. Then, switching on her sweetest smile, she picked up a dish and offered it to Dr. Blemish.

"Butter?" she said.

"Just a pat, thank you," Dr. Blemish replied, gazing at my mother while she, inspired by his attentiveness, proceeded to butter his roll. The two of them continued in this spellbound state until Dr. Blemish's gift-wrapped package tumbled from his lap to the floor.

"Oh," he said to me. "I almost forgot. This is for you."

Nobody has to ask me twice to open a present. This one turned out to be a brand new helmet. Shiny, purple, and flecked with silver, it looked like it belonged on a Hollywood stunt driver.

"Hey, thanks," I said. "This is cool."

"Wear it when you're riding your scooter," Dr. Blemish advised. "We don't want your mother to have to worry about you."

"Oh, Whitney," my mother said. "You're so thoughtful."

A Puff of Smoke

Pegasus is to ordinary scooters what the *Queen Mary* is to tugboats.

Bigger, more powerful, and beautiful in a grand and regal way, Pegasus represents a bold new way of thinking about personal transportation. With its twenty-four volt, twenty-four amp, three-hundred-watt rechargeable electric power system, Pegasus is quiet, reliable, and pollution-free. Outfitted with standard pneumatic ten-inch minibike tires, adjustable handlebars, independent suspension, and a surfboard-shaped platform nearly ten inches wide, Pegasus gets me where I'm going in comfort and style, while permitting me to stand up and see the sights along the way. The only serious drawback I can think of is that because Pegasus is battery powered, it's not advisable to take it out in the rain because there's a danger of electric shock. For me, however, this was only a theoretical concern, for since I first acquired my swift-winged companion, Mt. Mole hadn't seen a drop of rain — only a deluge of insects.

Scooting down Twelfth Street, en route to Mt. Mole Middle School, I brushed at a grasshopper on my shoulder. Immediately, it hopped onto my knuckles.

What a weird-looking creature, I thought.

His knobby knees are bigger than his feet, his

wings fold up like a golf umbrella, and his armored, bulgy-eyed head makes him look like someone wearing a safety helmet.

Like me, I thought.

Adjusting my new purple plastic headgear with one hand while steering Pegasus with the other, I wobbled to avoid a pothole.

Careful, I warned myself. *Don't shake up the passenger.*

In my backpack, nestled among my books and writing supplies, I carried Stony, his ice bucket terrarium topped with plastic wrap. After what the little crab had been through lately, I figured he might enjoy just hanging out with me—even if that meant going to school.

Of course, I should be looking for Mr. Farley, I thought.

Under normal conditions, you'd think that a school would be a good place to find an assistant principal. But these weren't normal conditions. For the next seven hours, my investigation was on hold.

At Twelfth and Lizard, in the center of the tornado-blasted area, I stopped to open a stick of gum. For some reason, chewing gum isn't allowed in school, so whatever chewing you hope to do must be done before you get there.

The day, warm and windy, seemed filled with promise. Where plush, green, carpetlike lawns had once demanded a ritual of fertilizing, sprinkling, weed-pulling, and mowing, unkempt clumps of native grasses swayed in the breeze. In the distance, against a blue, cloudless sky, Mt. Mole rose with the unwelcome presence of a fat man standing up in the front row at the movie. Knott Grande roosted like a turkey vulture on top.

"Doggone it, Andy!" a voice called. "You know as well as I do that this area is restricted."

Chief Eagle Talon stepped out of his Jeep.

"Morning, Chief," I said. "I'm just on my way to school."

"Well, take the Fifth Street detour, like everybody else," Chief Eagle Talon directed. "It'll be a long time before this part of town is safe."

"Okay," I agreed, crossing my fingers. "I won't do it again."

"Well, all right, then," the Chief responded. "See that you don't. We wouldn't want anything to happen to you."

"Speaking of things happening to people, Chief, " I said, "have you figured out anything about Mr. Farley?"

"Interesting you should ask," the Chief answered. "Just last night, I had two visions of Farley. In the first one, he was lying in a field shot head to toe with arrows. Until he opened his mouth and started insulting me, I was sure he was a porcupine."

"Hmmm," I said. "What do you think it means?"

"It could mean he's dead," the Chief answered,

scratching his head. "Or maybe it just means that I *wish* he were dead. He's got a way about him, you know?"

"So I've heard," I replied.

Chief Eagle Talon stretched his arms and yawned.

"You'd better go to school, now, Andy," he advised. "It's time I got back to my office."

"You mentioned two visions," I reminded him. "What was the other one?"

"Oh," the Chief answered. "In that one, Farley was sitting in a recliner, his hands and feet bound with duct tape. His mouth was taped shut, too — thank goodness. But the interesting part is that steam was coming out of his ears and sparks were shooting from his nose."

"That *is* interesting," I observed. "What do you make of it?"

"Hard to say," the Chief replied. "It could mean that Farley's still alive. Or it could mean to avoid eating Mexican food. With some visions, it's hard to be sure."

"Hmmm," I said, offering him a stick of gum. "Isn't it also possible that it means Mr. Farley's been kidnapped and he's steaming mad about it?"

"If he's alive, no matter what his circumstances, you can be sure he's mad about something," Chief Eagle Talon pointed out. "Anger is Farley's middle name."

He popped the gum into his mouth.

77

"At least he has one," I commented, thinking of my anonymous middle initial. "Anyway, maybe Mr. Farley has a lot to be mad about."

"Everybody's got a lot to be mad about," Chief Eagle Talon said. "The wise man learns to let it slide on by. Not Farley, though. That guy was a walking volcano."

At these words, a comic book image popped into my mind. Mr. Farley was walking down the hall of the middle school wearing a dark suit, a striped tie, and a grim, exaggerated frown—just his normal, everyday self—except that his head was cone-shaped, with flames and lava spewing from the top.

"Say—" I started.

But Chief Eagle Talon was already back in his Jeep. "Go to school," he ordered.

At Kingfisher Street, four blocks from the school's front door, I slowed to a stop. Kingfisher is the eastern border of the tornado-damaged area. When taken in a northerly direction, it eventually leads all the way to the top of the mountain, inspiring a few wiseacres to refer to it as Knott's driveway. Even by Mt. Mole standards, Kingfisher is a little-traveled street, since after approximately two meandering miles, it's blocked by a motorized metal gate with a sign from Knott Good Value Hardware that warns TRESPASSERS WILL BE PROSECUTED.

Mr. Knott knows everything that goes on in Mt. Mole, I said to myself. *I wonder what he might have heard about the comings and goings of Mr. Farley.*

My answer, it seemed, would have to wait, for suddenly, from deep inside my backpack, came a muffled, drumlike sound, a series of miniature explosions like popcorn popping in a pan. When I opened the flap, I found Stony jumping up and down inside his ice bucket, hitting his head against the taut plastic wrap. Again and again, as I watched in astonishment, he repeated his frantic actions — a creature crazed. If I hadn't known the little crustacean so well, I would have sworn he was a grasshopper.

In syncopation with Stony's strange bouncing, the earth itself began to shake, vibrating and trembling as if a great freight train were hurtling past. Clutching the terrarium to my chest, I dropped to the shifting ground as grasshoppers by the thousands leapt into the air and dogs across Mt. Mole howled in a mournful chorus.

The shaking subsided as quickly as it had begun, but in the next minute, a big, black, German-made sedan was roaring like an aftershock down Kingfisher Street, ignoring the Stop sign at the corner and passing within a few feet of me without slowing down. It was as if its occupants were running away from the mountain.

I could hear the bell ringing at school.

Am I late? I wondered. *Or has the bell been set off by the tremor?*

As if in reply, the mountain shuddered, gasped,

and coughed forth a spiraling plume of gray-white smoke. The thick stream was soon succeeded by a series of puffs — round, cloudlike clusters that vanished like runaway balloons.

Fascinated, I watched as more puffs appeared, this time in an orderly sequence. The first three were spherical in shape. The next three were short strokes of roughly equal length. These were followed by three more round ones.

Although I assumed that the phenomenon I was witnessing was natural, it nevertheless reminded me of smoke signals, the long-distance communication technique perfected by Native Americans.

Now if only I knew their secret code, I joked to myself.

"Andy, hurry up!" a voice called out.

Another car had appeared, the second in as many minutes.

Is Mt. Mole developing a traffic problem? I wondered.

Thankfully, this vehicle was more respectful of the speed limit than the one before. It also promised to be friendlier. Perky, blonde-haired Georgia Wayne was leaning from the window.

"That was the first bell, Andy!" she warned. "If you don't get a move on, you'll be sorry!"

Acknowledging her concern, I waved as she, too, passed by, leaving me to ponder my choices from within a cloud of parched prairie dust.

So what if I'm a few minutes late today? I thought. *Who would care?*

Certainly, not I. Not with a mountain calling me.

That was when it all came together in my head: Three short puffs. Three long puffs. Three short puffs.

"Wait a minute!" I said out loud to Stony. "I know this!"

It *was* code! I'd seen it in a movie from Hollywood Meets Mt. Mole: three shorts, three longs, three shorts. It's called Morse code, and the dots and dashes spelled out S O S—the international signal for distress! Someone on the mountain was signaling for help!

Trespassing or not, I thought, *it's time to pay a visit to Knott Grande!*

Word Power

There used to be a flower shop on the northeast corner where Kingfisher crosses Third. But when it closed its doors for good, the location was taken over by a combination allergy clinic and pet store run by Mrs. Stitch's younger half-sister, Miss Fleece.

A registered nurse, Miss Fleece had left her job at Mt. Mole Goodness and Mercy Hospital following an unfortunate mix-up involving a doctor's scrawled medical instructions and a supervisor's order for a carry-out pizza. One man nearly died as a result of her error — Mt. Mole's only published author, an elderly and reclusive children's novelist named Daschell Potts.

I mention the Potts episode because it was Miss Fleece whom Pegasus, Stony, and I accidentally ran down as we were racing toward the mountain, and she, after yet another fitful night of guilt-ridden sleep, was just arriving at work, the keys to her shop clutched in her hand.

Apparently, even at fifteen miles an hour, an object in motion colliding with one that's half-asleep can still cause plenty of damage. Luckily for me, I was wearing a helmet — the gift from Dr. Blemish — but Stony's ice bucket was not, nor was the unprotected Miss Fleece, who dropped a jarful of newly gathered wolf spiders onto the pavement. In her haste to escape the surging, hairy sea of irritated arachnids, Miss Fleece twisted her ankle.

As to whether my actions were reckless or I was an unwitting instrument of karmic justice, I'm sure I'll never know. But the spider-scooter collision, as accidents always do, changed my plans for the rest of the day. Instead of storming the castle at the top of Mt. Mole, I spent the next hour and fifteen minutes answering questions from Chief Eagle Talon, who wasn't buying any part of my story about the S O S.

"Don't tell *me* about Indian smoke signals!" he intoned. "I *know!*"

"Whether you believe it or not," I insisted, "that mountain is calling me!"

"Well, of course, it is," Chief Eagle Talon replied. "It's where you were born. But that's not an acceptable reason to skip school."

"I was what?" I said.

But the Chief, shutting the door to his Jeep, had terminated the conversation. With his eagle eyes on my back all along the way, I drove my scooter and my hermit crab to school.

"Where've you been?" Georgia whispered.

I was taking my customary seat in the front row of English class, a spot that I require so I can read Miss Futon's tiny handwriting. At that time Georgia was seated directly behind me.

"You missed roll call, team-building exercises, weekly review, and tomorrow's assignment," she said, ticking them off on her fingers. "My gosh, Andy, are you just looking for trouble?"

"It couldn't be helped," I explained. "I was responding to a mayday from the mountain."

"I see," Georgia responded, obviously skeptical.

"I'm not kidding, Georgia!" I cried, turning around in my chair.

"Andy Forrest!" Miss Futon snapped. "Perhaps you'd find it harder to interrupt this class if we were taking a pop quiz."

"Oh, that's not necessary," I replied.

But like many people who announce ideas without

thinking them through, Miss Futon feared losing face if she backed off.

"Everyone put away your books," she instructed, "and get out pencil and paper."

Glaring at me, the class groaned in unison.

"Sorry," I mouthed, shrugging my shoulders.

"We have twenty-five minutes," Miss Futon said. "Enough time for you to provide complete definitions for ten vocabulary words."

Again, the class moaned. Whatever popularity I might once have enjoyed was now gone.

Miss Futon flipped open a fat, tattered dictionary, sending a dozing grasshopper skittering across the freshly waxed floor. With her index finger, she stabbed at a page, read the result, and posted it on the board. One by one, a list of words appeared, each presented in her compressed, minuscule, nearly illegible script:

APHORISM
CASTIGATE
DISCORDANT
DUPLICITY
EXOSKELETON
KNOLL
PERMUTATION
PRODIGIOUS
PROMONTORY
VULCANOLOGY

Well, I thought, *so much for getting an A on* this *test!*

Although several of the words seemed familiar, the only ones whose definitions I was sure of were "exoskeleton" (the hard outer shell found on crabs, grasshoppers, and certain other invertebrates) and "knoll" (a topographical rise, or hill). "Duplicity" sounded like one I ought to know, but, unfortunately, at that particular moment, I didn't.

And what about this word "vulcanology"? I wondered. *Why does it keep following me around?*

With a long, audible sigh of resignation, I clicked my ballpoint pen into action, licked the tip, and proceeded to do what I've done so many times before — I guessed at the answers. When the bell signaled time was up, I was just finishing.

"Vulcanology," I scribbled hastily. "The study of Vulcans."

Somehow this didn't seem like enough, so I added more words until the definition read: "Vulcanology. The study of Vulcans — their social structure, customs, and philosophy."

"Well, that was certainly a swell way to restart school," a sarcastic Georgia Wayne complained, stuffing her books into her locker. "Why'd you have to go and do that?"

"It's not my fault," I said, cradling Stony and his ice bucket underneath my arm. "I've got higher priorities. I've got to go to the mountain."

"Where you have to go is your next class," Georgia corrected me. She kicked her locker shut. "Remember, Andy?" she said, tapping my forehead with her knuckles. "We're in school."

"This is more important than school," I insisted. "This is . . ." I struggled to find just the right word. "Prodigious!"

"You don't even know what that word means," Georgia scoffed.

"It's not important what a word means," I replied. "What matters is how it sounds when you use it. It's a basic principle of Vulcan philosophy. You'd know this if you'd studied Vulcanology."

"Vulcanology?" Georgia repeated. "Good grief, Andy, sometimes the way you think is as sloppy as how you dress! Vulcanology has nothing to do with word usage. Vulcanology is the study of volcanoes."

"It is?" I said.

"Well, of course, it is!" Georgia affirmed. "The term comes from Vulcan, blacksmith to the Roman gods. Long ago, people thought Vulcan lived deep inside Vulcano, an island in the Mediterranean Sea that was an active volcano. These days, vulcanology is also known as volcanology, with an 'o' instead of a 'u.' Either spelling is correct."

I stood staring at Georgia Wayne with my mouth wide open. This was embarrassing!

"Volcanoes?" I nearly squeaked the word. "Are you sure?"

"Do I look like someone who isn't sure?" Georgia replied. "Give me a break! I learned that one in sixth grade."

She narrowed her blue eyes into a hawklike squint.

"That was at my old school," she added. "Before I had the misfortune to move to Mt. Mole."

Suddenly, my brain began operating at the speed of a supercomputer. In a matter of milliseconds, it reviewed the pertinent facts:

One: Assistant Principal Farley disappears under suspicious circumstances, his last known actions having to do with vulcanology.

Two: Before you can say, "Jack Spratt," the Mt. Mole Chamber of Commerce — Lucius Knott, president — dismisses the case at a town meeting.

Three: Rumblings and explosions are heard coming from Mt. Mole, Mr. Knott's private mountain, not to mention that the mountain appears to be expanding.

Four: For Sale signs pop up on Mr. Knott's businesses like blisters on a sunburned pig.

Five: Using smoke signals, somebody on the mountain broadcasts a cry for help.

Six: Vulcanology is revealed to be the study of volcanoes.

Seven: I should learn to pay attention!

Setting Stony's ice bucket atop the lockers, I grabbed Georgia by the shoulders and looked her square in the eye, my prominent nose in direct contact with her small, pert, freckled one.

"You've got to believe me," I said. "This *is* prodigious. This is the most prodigious thing that's ever happened in Mt. Mole, and you and I are right in the middle of it."

Georgia neither looked away nor sought to slip from my grasp.

"Explain yourself," she ordered.

"Well," I proceeded slowly, "unless I'm completely mistaken, Mr. Knott is holding Mr. Farley prisoner on the mountain."

"Prisoner?" she repeated.

"That's right," I replied. "But wait, there's more. That mountain—maybe you should be sitting down for this—that mountain, that modest, unassuming hill known as Mt. Mole, is no ordinary mountain. It's a direct pipeline to our unstable earth's violent, boiling core. In other words, my dear, Mt. Mole is a volcano!"

As if to punctuate my revelation, from the top of the lockers came a rapid, rhythmic, *pip-pip-pip* noise, like someone tapping on the window. It was, however, a terrified hermit crab slamming his tiny body against a barrier of plastic wrap.

"What's that?" Georgia asked.

"It's Stony," I replied, quickly retrieving the terrarium. "The last time he acted like this, there was an earthquake, or something very much like it, centered at the mountain. He seems to sense underground activity before it happens."

Georgia looked into the ice bucket.

"I didn't know crabs could jump," she said.

"Most can't," I admitted. "It's one of many skills that makes Stony so special."

"I see," Georgia observed, as Stony continued to bounce like a paddleball on a rubber band. "So he's more than a pet—he's a seismograph."

Lending weight to her conclusion, a low, muffled blast rose from the distant knoll of Mt. Mole, followed by another, and another, each at roughly equal intervals.

BOOM, BOOM, BOOM, BOOM.

It was as if the mountain were trying out for the Mt. Mole Middle School Marching Band.

Recruiting a Partner

There are two kinds of people in this world.

There are those who, on learning that a nearby hill has become an active volcano, cry, "Let's get out of here!"

And there are others, whose interests include saving people who may be in danger, who say, "Let's go up there!"

I was surprised to learn that while I represented the

second group, Georgia was a charter member of the first.

"Are you nuts, Andy?" she exclaimed when I proposed that the two of us take off for Mt. Mole. "You've never even set foot on that stupid speed bump. Why would you want to start now?"

"Actually," I corrected her, "according to Chief Eagle Talon, I was up there nearly thirteen years ago. But today's reason is because that's where Mr. Farley is—at least, that's what I think. Anyway, I can't run out on my hometown at the first sign of trouble."

"The first sign?" Georgia retorted, shaking a grasshopper from her hair. "You call that volcano the first sign? This sad sack, backprairie town's been advertising trouble ever since I arrived. Tornadoes, drought, insect plagues, unsolved crimes, and a rapidly shrinking population that ought to be in a loony bin. And now it dawns on you that that overblown carbuncle out there is in danger of exploding? Give me a break, Andy! That's hardly what I'd call the first sign of trouble. In fact, as far as I'm concerned, it's the last. Count me out!"

"But, Georgia," I protested. "I need you."

"Forget it, Andy!" Georgia said, her blue eyes flashing. "You know what your trouble is? You've lived here too long. You think Mt. Mole is normal."

Ouch! I thought.

"Please, Georgia," I begged. "I can't save Mr. Farley all by myself."

"But why me?" she asked. "Shouldn't you be recruiting an adult?"

"All the adults all suspects!" I cried out. "Even my mother!"

Georgia's face softened. Sensing an opportunity, I tried a fresh approach.

"Look at it like this," I suggested. "What better way to satisfy your curiosity about Mt. Mole?"

"Sorry," Georgia replied, shifting her schoolbooks from one hip to the other, "but I'm not at all curious to find out what volcanoes look like close up — if that's what that absurd blister really is."

"Well, of course, it's a volcano," I claimed. "But it's not like we're in danger. Even you have said that Mt. Mole is tiny for a mountain. That makes it tiny for a volcano, too."

"Tiny for a volcano, but for a bomb, it's enormous," Georgia pointed out, "and I don't intend to be standing on it when it goes off."

"We'll have Stony with us," I reminded her. "He'll be our early-warning system."

"Forget it!" Georgia said. "I'm not putting my life in the hands of any creature whose brain weighs less than a fingernail clipping, thank you very much. Besides, I have cheerleading practice after school."

"If we take Pegasus, we can be there and back in no time," I said.

"I'm sorry, Andy," Georgia replied. "I'd like to help you, but daring rescues of bad-tempered strangers trapped on ticking time bombs aren't my style."

Impulsively, I blurted out, "I'll let you drive."

In the heat of the moment, I'd defied my own rule about Pegasus, but my instincts proved a better judge of the situation than my reason. The effect on Georgia was immediate. Her eyes opened wide like a comic book close-up.

Be cool, Andy, I advised myself. *This is a game of skill.*

"You'd let me drive your scooter?" Georgia asked, incredulous. "That black lightning bolt with the mythological name? The one that's your true best friend?"

"If Pegasus came with keys," I told her, "I'd hand them over now."

Georgia chewed her lower lip as opposing forces battled it out within her. When at last she spoke, the hunger in her voice was unmistakable. Underneath that pretty, pampered exterior beat the heart of a scooter chick.

"Where will you be?" she asked.

"I'll be right behind you," I answered. "Holding on for dear life."

"All right," Georgia agreed. "I'll do it. But not until cheerleading practice is over."

"But—" I said, meaning, What if Mr. Farley is near death's door? What if Mr. Knott is on his way back to Knott Grande? What if the mountain really is about to explode? What if I get cold feet and change my mind?

"Take it or leave it," Georgia demanded.

"I'll take it," I agreed.

"Fine," Georgia said. "Have Pegasus outside the gym at four o' clock. And don't forget to bring something to eat. I get hungry after school."

I watched as the girl of my dreams disappeared down the hallway.

Well, I thought. *That wasn't so difficult.*

Store of Knowledge

For gifted students in danger of becoming bored, Mt. Mole Middle School created an accelerated learning program called Pursuing Individual Goals. This was an unfortunate choice of phrase, in my opinion, since cumbersome official names have a way of becoming catchy acronyms — in this case, the initials spelled PIG. So this year, when three of us were chosen to participate, it was inevitable that the other kids would dub us "the three little pigs."

They should have saved their breath. PIG is hardly worth the trouble. In fact, in my experience, it's little more than a semiprivate study hall. Nevertheless, for an hour after lunch every school day, I'm required to sit in the library with a couple of affable nerds while a teacher hovers nearby to answer our questions, most often consisting of "What time is it?" and "May I go to the bathroom?" and "What time is it now?"

On this occasion, I took advantage of my book-rich surroundings to learn more about volcanoes. What I discovered came as a surprise to me. As it turns out, not all volcanoes behave like Fourth of July fireworks. In fact, volcanoes come in as many different varieties as donuts.

Some volcanoes do blow up, like in comics, throwing fireballs from their mouths and obliterating native villages. But many volcanoes never explode, they just ooze molten rock, frequently from a variety of openings, for days, months, or even years on end. Other volcanoes simply pass gas from time to time.

There are deadly gas-passers that belch hot, poisonous fumes into the air without warning that wipe out everything that walks, crawls, or flies for miles downwind. There are others that release plain, ordinary steam at predictable intervals, much like the tourist-friendly geysers found in national parks. And there are volcanoes that exhibit combinations of these eruption styles.

Earthquakes often accompany volcanic activity, but not always. Volcanoes can be thousands of feet high, or they can rise up overnight from the sea floor, the desert, or flat farmland. Most volcanoes on earth have been identified and are associated with well-mapped subterranean areas, but every once in a while a new volcano appears where it's least expected.

When taken by surprise in this manner, vulcanologists rarely admit, "We had no idea that this would happen." Instead, they say, "This event contributes to our store of knowledge."

As my hour of independent study progressed, I began to understand that the earth is not the permanent place I'd supposed it to be. There's simply no such thing as solid rock. Beneath the floating, broken pie crust we're standing on is an incredibly hot ocean of magma, a pressurized vat of liquid rock that's constantly seeking new ways to reach the surface.

Everything, it turns out, is in a constant state of change. Everything in the universe, whether living or not, is in the process of becoming something else. Nothing—nothing at all—is standing still.

The Play's the Thing

The closest thing to recess at Mt. Mole Middle School is Mrs. Bagelbottom's drama class, an unstructured playground for the mind that comes right after PIG. Today, it promised to be especially interesting. Mrs. Bagelbottom was assigning parts for her new play.

Previewed at the town meeting, *Montaña del Oro —The Mountain of Gold* was a dramatic invention about Spanish explorer Francisco Vásquez de

Coronado's search for Quivira, a legendary city of gold. Coronado's expedition into the heart of the North American continent in 1541 was destined to be his last, netting him not so much as a single peso, but, fortunately for modern-day Mt. Moleans, at the very point where he and his men decided to turn back, Coronado "discovered" Mt. Mole.

"I took a few liberties with the facts," Mrs. Bagelbottom confessed, "but I left the truth intact."

Given its historical importance to Mt. Moleans, *Montaña del Oro — The Mountain of Gold* seemed likely to become as revered a tradition as the town pageants commemorating the Fourth of July, Thanksgiving, and Mr. Knott's birthday. Thus, despite its possible shortcomings, the play's debut performance was practically guaranteed to be a sellout. To be chosen for a role was indeed an honor.

"Here," Mrs. Bagelbottom instructed. "Try this on."

Unpacking a carton from a New York City costume shop, my drama teacher handed me a silver metal helmet with a wide, curved brim and a high, peaked crown. Every square inch of the strange-looking headgear was sculpted with squiggles, circles, stars, and swirls. To my untutored eye, it looked like a Jell-O mold, and a small one at that, but, anxious to please, I forced it onto my head.

"It's a replica of a sixteenth-century Spanish conquistador's helmet," Mrs. Bagelbottom explained. "It was expensive, but worth it, I think. Success is in the details."

"It's a little snug," I reported.

"Hmmm," Mrs. Bagelbottom mused. "It's supposed to slip on easily. When was the last time you had a haircut?"

"I don't remember," I replied.

"That could be the problem," she speculated. "Oh, well. Give it to me and I'll see if the custodian can enlarge it."

"It won't come off," I told her.

"What do you mean?" Mrs. Bagelbottom asked.

"It's stuck," I said. "I can't get it off my head."

"Let me try," she directed, giving the helmet a Bagelbottom-size tug.

"Ow!" I cried. "You're scalping me!"

Mrs. Bagelbottom finally released her grip, and I collapsed like a scarecrow.

"Well, I'll be . . ." my drama teacher mused, offering me her hand. "I'm sure the brochure explicitly stated, 'One Size Fits All.'"

"I'm a gifted student," I pointed out, standing up to dust off my jeans. "Maybe my brain is bigger than average."

"I suppose that is altogether possible," Mrs. Bagelbottom conceded.

"Unfortunately," I continued, "it's not big enough to figure out how to get this thing off."

"Well, whatever you do," Mrs. Bagelbottom

pleaded, "don't damage it. It's the only one we have."

"I'll keep that in mind," I replied.

For the remainder of the hour, we practiced the scene where it dawns on Coronado that's he's been duped by the wily Indians and there is no city of gold.

"My first thought was, he lied in every word," I recited, grimacing in pain from the too-tight helmet. Mrs. Bagelbottom clapped her hands. "Your expression is perfect, Andy," she said. "Remember to do it like that in the performance."

The last class of the day was consumer science, a mandatory course of study invented by school officials to eliminate the last remaining social differences between the sexes. During the previous semester, boys and girls were taught the arcane techniques of sewing. Now, the focus was on cooking. Interestingly, although classes were led by volunteers from throughout Mt. Mole, all were women. Today's instructor was Marianne Fernelle. The food she presented was popcorn.

What a coincidence, I thought, greeting her with a nod of my helmet, as a few kids snickered behind their hands.

"Popcorn originated in the Americas," the Fernelle twin announced, coughing to clear her raspy voice. "When the Europeans arrived, the Native Americans were cultivating as many as seven hundred different varieties. All have one thing in common. When heated to a temperature of four hundred degrees Fahrenheit, the stuff explodes — don't ask me why."

From the back of the room, a hand shot up, its owner one of my compatriots from PIG.

"I said don't ask me why," Marianne repeated.

"It's because water vapor trapped inside the kernel is converted to steam," my PIG partner felt compelled to explain. "The heat increases the water's volume some fifteen hundred times, which blasts the kernel open, turning it inside out to produce the light, fluffy food we know as popcorn."

"Okay, thanks a lot," Marianne said, rolling her eyes.

But the PIG kid wasn't finished. "The process works like a volcano," he went on, "except that in addition to water vapor, in a volcano you've got carbon dioxide, sulfur dioxide, hydrogen sulfide, and other gases bursting from lava to form a porous, air-filled rock. Still, it's accurate to say that both volcanic rock and popcorn have been 'gas-popped.'"

"Okey-dokey," Marianne replied. "If you say so. But if I was home watching a movie, I don't think I'd be cooking myself any tub of hot, buttered rock."

At this, the boys and girls broke into laughter. I, however, didn't crack a smile. My mind had moved on to another subject.

Mr. Farley must have known this, I reasoned.

Could it be why he had popcorn on his pajamas?

But even as I posed the question, I knew I couldn't answer it.

Part of my problem, I realized, was that I was losing confidence. Before the mystery in Mt. Mole began, I'd considered myself to be a pretty brainy guy. Now, I was beginning to get an idea of how much I didn't know—and I don't just mean other people's secrets. It took Georgia Wayne to set me straight on vulcanology, and it was a fellow PIG who made the connection between popcorn and volcanoes. How many other Mt. Moleans were walking around with knowledge I'd never bothered to acquire?

It was a humbling experience, and because the thought process resembled philosophizing, it was nearly an injurious one, as well. Walking out of consumer science class, I accidentally slammed into a locker door left open in the hall. Only Mrs. Bagelbottom's one-size-too-small conquistador helmet saved me from a concussion.

A Sudden Insight

Although considered part of Mt. Mole Middle School, the Lucius Knott Center for Athletic Competition is located two and a half blocks from the rest of the campus, sprawling like a discount superstore at Fourteenth and Groundhog. Perhaps school officials reasoned that the farther kids have to walk, the more physically fit they'll get. If so, they'd failed with me. Until I got Pegasus, I avoided any school activity that required a hike to the gym.

I consulted my watch. It was 3:15; I had plenty of time before I was scheduled to meet Georgia.

Maybe I'll get some snacks, I thought.

I flipped Pegasus's power switch from "O" to "I." For some reason, with electronic devices, whereas "O" logically stands for "off," "I" is the designation for "on." I made a mental note to ask my PIG teacher why. There's so much that I don't know.

Pegasus seemed raring to go, leaping up the moment my sneaker touched the footboard, heading intuitively toward the Mt. Mole Mini Mart at the corner of Tenth and Chipmunk. With Mrs. Bagelbottom's conquistador helmet stuck firmly on my head, my racing helmet dangled unused from Pegasus's handlebars, while inside my backpack, my hermit crab drummed ominously, like a jungle warrior signaling an attack.

"Settle down, Stony," I advised. "You're going to hurt yourself."

Stony's increased restlessness was not a good sign, but I was not planning to mention this to Georgia. After all, hadn't I already explained to her, hours before, that we'd better hurry? She was the one who had revised the timetable.

One by one, at equal intervals, the north-south streets of Mt. Mole whizzed beneath my feet: Groundhog, Flea, Eagle, Dog. I marveled at how they followed the neat, geometric pattern of a checkerboard, a ticktacktoe game, a rabbit fence, a tattersall plaid.

Mt. Mole is such an orderly, well-plotted town, I observed. *Unlike nature, which is fundamentally unruly.*

From the mountain came the sound of distant thunder.

"That had better be rain," I said.

But I knew that it wasn't. It was the mountain.

Why had I been so slow to catch on?

I wondered how I ever got picked for PIG. Not only did I have a lot to learn, most of what I *had* figured out had come too late to do me much good. For example, it wasn't until I was back outside the Mt. Mole Mini Mart, having purchased a bagful of candy and a six-pack of soda pop from a man who admired my conquistador helmet, that I grasped the significance of what earlier had ambled so anonymously through my inattentive brain:

Equally spaced crisscrossing lines.

Tattersall plaid.

When it arrived, the insight struck with the force of a juice-filled grasshopper flying smack against my poor, thick head: The streets of Mt. Mole were laid out like the pattern on Mr. Farley's pajamas!

And that's not all.

When discovered on the floor in his living room, Mr. Farley's pajamas were covered with popcorn, a substance that's formed in the same way as volcanic rock.

Bingo! I thought.

Suddenly, the explanation was as plain as the prominent nose on Mr. Farley's face. He *had* been conducting an experiment! The whole thing—the mound of popcorn, the pajamas—was a scale model. Mr. Farley had been trying to predict the effects of a volcanic blast on the town of Mt. Mole!

Don't kick me out of PIG right away, I thought. *There's hope for me yet!*

Snow Falling on Scooters

I couldn't wait to tell Georgia.

With its soft whine punctuated by the intermittent snaps and pops of grasshoppers being crunched beneath its tires, Pegasus poured on the power, racing like the wind to Knott Athletic.

Georgia was waiting outside the gym, dressed in the green and gray uniform of a Mt. Mole Middle School cheerleader, her arms folded across her embroidered "M," her sneaker-clad foot tapping impatiently on the parking lot pavement.

"Where've you been?" she demanded. "And why

do you have a torpedo on your head?"

"Here," I replied, offering her a chocolate-nut-nougat bar like you'd present raw hamburger to a growling dog. "I brought you candy. Also, you might want to wear this while you're driving."

I handed Georgia the helmet from Dr. Blemish.

"Thanks," she said, tucking her blonde hair underneath the shiny purple plastic. Tentatively, she stepped onto Pegasus's footboard and grasped the controls. "Now what do I do?"

"The basic idea with any two-wheeler is to keep it upright and balanced," I explained. "Pegasus likes to run at top speed, which you accomplish by squeezing the caliper on your right as far as it will go. To stop, just release it, and squeeze the one on your left."

"Sounds simple enough," Georgia said. "Here goes!"

"Don't you want to practice first?" I asked.

"Don't be silly, Andy," she replied. "It's a scooter, not an airplane."

On the word "airplane," Pegasus sprang to life and lurched away with Georgia at the helm, her expression like that of a jungle cat suddenly freed from its cage.

"Hey, wait up!" I hollered, sprinting after them as they zipped across the parking lot toward Heron Road.

On my back was a canvas pack weighing at least thirty pounds—books and school supplies, soda pop, candy, and a prognosticating hermit crab being jostled into a permanent state of submission. In no time at all, the distance between the runner and the runaways widened. Soon Pegasus and Georgia were out of sight.

Maybe avoiding the gym wasn't such a great idea, I thought, panting.

Hitching up my backpack, I began walking. It was another beautiful day in Mt. Mole. Outlined against the cloudless sky, the trees seemed drawn in pen and ink. On the sidewalk far ahead, two identically shaped people were out for a stroll. It wasn't until I arrived at Eighth Street, where our paths met, that I was able to recognize them as the Fernelles.

"Why the hat?" quizzed Marianne. "Expecting trouble?"

"Not exactly," I replied. "Have you seen a girl on an electric scooter?"

"Does she zigzag when she goes down the road?" asked Doug.

"Like a sidewinder on wheels?" added Marianne.

"That's the one," I said. "Which way did she go?"

"This way," Doug answered, pointing west toward Ibis Street.

"And that way," his sister added, pointing north toward the mountain.

"She seemed to be having difficulty controlling her machine," Doug observed, adjusting his toupee.

"Or making up her mind," suggested Marianne,

her voice rising at least a full octave.

"Careful, sister," warned Doug, flashing her a conspiratorial look.

Instantly, an exchange with Dr. Blemish came to mind.

"Mt. Mole is more like a family than a town," I'd told him.

"A family with plenty of family secrets," he'd replied.

Hmmm, I thought, as the twins scurried down the sidewalk.

Mentally flipping a coin, I continued to Seventh Street before turning west again at the South Groundhog branch of Knott Secure Savings. Encountering no one, I crossed Ibis and was just approaching Jackalope when, to my astonishment, snow began to fall.

Snow? I thought. *In April?*

A spring snowfall is not entirely unheard of on the plains, but on the few occasions in recorded history when it has occurred, the temperature was considerably colder than it was now. According to the digital sign I'd passed at Mr. Knott's bank, it was a balmy sixty-seven degrees in Mt. Mole.

How can this be? I wondered.

But thoughts of my hometown's quirky weather were quickly displaced by a familiar electrical whine. With relief, I looked up to see Pegasus and Georgia approaching.

"This is so cool!" Georgia gushed, slowing down too late to keep the scooter's front tire from bouncing off the curb. "I have *got* to get one of these!"

"I don't know why," I muttered. "It doesn't seem to bother you to take mine all over town."

"I want to get a new one," she said. "This one has scratches."

Georgia removed her helmet and fluffed her hair with her fingertips.

"Do they come in yellow?" she asked.

"Probably," I answered. "But have you forgotten we're on a mission? While you're out joyriding, time is running out for Mr. Farley. If it weren't for the Fernelles, I'd still be looking for you."

"The who?" Georgia asked.

"The Fernelle twins," I explained. "You passed them on the road."

"Oh," she replied. "You mean that pair where the brother is obviously disguised as the sister and the sister as the brother? Yeah, I remember them. What a couple of doofuses!"

At this unexpected revelation, I did a doubletake.

"The Fernelles have traded places?" I said, shaking my head. "But why would they want to do that?"

"Oh, for heaven's sake, Andy, don't you know anything?" Georgia chided. "They're twins! It's a tradition. They do it because they can!"

Good grief! I thought. *What else have I missed?*

Humiliated, I stared at the ground. The unseasonable snowfall had begun to turn the gutters of Jackalope Street a pale, deathly gray.

"We better get a move on," I said. "Do you want me to drive?"

"No way," she replied. "A deal is a deal. Hop on back."

But before I could carry out Georgia's instructions, a woman's voice stopped me.

"Andy!" it shouted. "Isn't this terrible!"

In my excitement at catching up with the runaways, I'll failed to realize we were parked in front of my English teacher's house. I turned to see Miss Futon opening the front door for Vesuvius, who descended the steps with the painstaking stiffness of a rusted robot.

"Hello, Miss Futon," I called. "Nice weather we're having."

Jumping over her dog, Miss Futon hurried to the curb.

"Oh, Andy," she lamented, worried furrows forming on her forehead. "This isn't weather. It's volcanic ash. It's coming from the mountain — just as Jacob predicted."

Huh? I thought. *Ash? Mountain? Mr. Farley?*

Is there a psychological condition in which a person feels he's always the last to know? There must be! I made a mental note to ask Dr. Blemish what it's called.

"Andy and I are headed up there right now,"

Georgia blurted out. "He thinks that's where the kidnappers have taken Mr. Farley."

Dang! I thought.

With the swift, sure force of a red-tailed hawk nailing a prairie vole, I shot Georgia a look. Obviously, she wasn't from Mt. Mole. She couldn't keep a secret.

"We were just kicking around a few ideas," I attempted to explain. "One of us happened to mention the mountain. We probably won't be going there at all."

But Miss Futon wasn't buying my cover-up. When she spoke, it wasn't what I wanted to hear.

"Take Vesuvius with you," she directed. "He can help find Jacob. I'd go myself, but I promised Mrs. Bagelbottom I'd accompany her to the dedication at the depot."

I watched as her creaky old dog peed on a flower.

"If it's all the same to you, Miss Futon," I said, "I don't think we have that kind of time. The sun's going to be setting in a couple of hours."

"He'll *save* you time," Miss Futon insisted. "Dogs have a very advanced sense of smell, and Vesuvius is familiar with Jacob's scent."

"Do it, Andy," Georgia urged. "He's so cute."

"I don't know," I responded. "This scooter goes pretty fast. Do you think Vesuvius can keep up?"

"He's always been very determined," Miss Futon answered.

"I'll drive in circles," Georgia quietly offered.

"That should at least make it easier for him."

Why do girls do this? I wondered. *Why do they always take each other's side?*

"Okay," I agreed. "But we have to hurry."

"Just let me run inside," Miss Futon said. "I'll get one of Jacob's socks."

Socks? I thought.

"Why would I want to wear Mr. Farley's socks?" I asked.

To her credit, Georgia merely rolled her eyes.

Crossing Over

Of course, it turned out that the purpose of the sock was to get Vesuvius's sniffer onto the right scent.

I'm sure that if I hadn't had so much on my mind, I would've figured this out by the time Pegasus pulled away from the curb. As it was, I was so preoccupied with holding on to Georgia as she wobbled and wove down the road that it wasn't until we were halfway down Kingfisher that I finally put two and two together.

"Oh, I get it," I said, once again the last to know. "When we get to the mountain, we'll let Vesuvius take a whiff of this."

"Is he still back there?" Georgia called over her shoulder.

"I think so," I replied, squinting to make out a

motionless shape a hundred yards behind us. "Either that or someone's run over a possum."

"Maybe you should swap with him," Georgia suggested.

"I beg your pardon?" I replied.

Despite the motion sickness caused by Georgia's driving, I was starting to enjoy the ride, especially since it required me to keep my hands around her waist.

"We'll make better time if Vesuvius rides while you run beside us," she explained.

"Now, wait just a minute," I complained. "I'm not unwilling to compromise to rescue Mr. Farley, but giving up my spot for Miss Futon's dog? I'm sorry, but no."

With an impact that knocked me from my perch, Georgia ran Pegasus into the curb. To my added discomfort, I saw that she'd come to a stop in front of Miss Fleece's pet store and allergy clinic, scene of my accident earlier in the day. Judging from the traffic going west on Third Street, it was near closing time. I hoped Miss Fleece had already gone home.

"Now, you listen to me, Andy Forrest," Georgia commanded, lightning flashing from her eyes. "We're all having to make sacrifices here. Get that dog and put him on this scooter before I change my mind about this whole thing."

Trudging down Kingfisher to collect Vesuvius, it struck me how little control we have over our lives.

Outside forces always have the upper hand. Many times they're natural in origin, such as when tornadoes strike, insects invade, or volcanoes threaten to erupt. These I can understand — sort of. It's the other kind I find so bewildering, the kind in which we have to submit to the whims of certain people.

I wondered, *Who put them in charge?*

Once again, my philosophizing brought swift and certain punishment. When I picked him up, Vesuvius bit me on the hand.

Dang and double-dang! I thought.

I scooped up that ornery, over-the-hill stinkpot, hauled him all the way back to Third Street, and plopped him like a bagful of potting soil onto the footboard of the scooter.

"Here," I said to Georgia. "Now, let's get going."

As we waited to cross the street, a station wagon with an official state seal drove by. Behind the wheel, the gray streak in his hair identifying him as surely as Third Street's painted centerline, was Dr. Blemish. Cuddled up beside him, too close to be wearing a seat belt, was my mother.

"That psychologist must be pretty good at his job," Georgia observed. "Your mother doesn't appear to be troubled at all."

My mother's eyes flickered briefly toward Pegasus, but she failed to recognize the glum-faced conquistador standing with the cheerleader and the broken-down dog.

People see what they expect to see, I thought.

This explained why no one else was concerned about the strange sights and sounds coming from the mountain. Except for Mr. Farley and Miss Futon, it would no more occur to a Mt. Molean that their mountain is a volcano than it would that their chief of police is not a policeman.

The facts can't compete with the familiar.

By the time our caravan resumed its journey, the snowy dusting from the mountain had ceased, having been succeeded by a drifting cloud of volcanic steam. As I searched in this mist for any decipherable sequence of dots and dashes, I was surprised to see it mingle with a second, more forceful cloud rising up from somewhere to our left.

"Good grief!" I exclaimed, chasing after Pegasus as Georgia and Vesuvius sped across Second Street. "Not another volcano!"

"Maybe this would be a good time to consult your crab!" Georgia called over her shoulder.

"Stony's traumatized," I replied, grasping a Stop sign while I caught my breath. "At the moment, he's completely useless."

"Looks like he isn't the only one," Georgia muttered.

But as soon as we reached First Street, the source of the second cloud became clear.

"Look!" I cried. "It's coming from the tracks."

Parked at historic Mt. Mole Depot, puffing as

noisily as it had in the 1880s, was a steam locomotive, the steamer that Earl and his fellow railroad preservationists had been working to restore. Although a small engine by modern standards, its wide, black funnel released so much ash, smoke, and steam that the cloud from the mountain was completely obscured.

A crowd was gathering at the station — Chief Eagle Talon, Mrs. Stitch, Miss Fleece, Dr. Blemish, my mother, the Fernelles, and many others.

"This could work to our advantage," I said.

"How's that?" Georgia asked.

"Everyone's busy with the train," I explained. "They won't notice us."

Between downtown Mt. Mole and the mountain with the same name there is nothing but the plains, a vast, fertile home to more than seventy-five types of grasses and countless varieties of wildflowers that bloom from April through October. Usually, this patch of prairie is a peaceful place, a sanctuary, quiet and sublimely beautiful, conducive to nature study, painting, reading, and meditation. But not this time.

Boulders, many as big as farm animals, were rolling across the road like tumbleweeds in the wind.

"There's no time to lose!" I cried.

Georgia poured on the power. Like the great winged stallion it was named for, Pegasus leapt nimbly and surely ahead, dodging rocks with effortless ease. For once, my colleague's zigzag style of driving

114

made sense. I, on the other hand, jumping, weaving, and racing to keep up, quickly fell behind. Soon, Georgia, Pegasus, and Vesuvius were out of sight.

"Hey, wait up!" I cried.

But mine was a voice crying in the wilderness, a wilderness in which the grasshoppers, always numerous, had become as thick as hailstones. The bug-eyed army darkened the skies and clung to my conquistador helmet like honeybees swarming on a hive. Through the dense curtain of insects and smoke, the indistinct outline of Knott Grande undulated like a ghost ship adrift in a stormy sea.

Somewhere up there, I thought, *Mr. Farley is locked in a tower or chained to a dungeon wall!*

Through sheer effort of will, I pressed on, up the side of a mountain that seemed to know I was coming. With each step, the barrage intensified — boulders hurtled across the roadway and rocks, like errant golf balls, whistled past my ears and ricocheted off my helmet.

This is harder than I thought it'd be, I told myself.

Suddenly, like a flag waving through the smoke of battle, Pegasus's handlebars appeared, then its footboard, then its tires, and finally Georgia, who was sitting beside the scooter eating a candy bar.

"Oh, there you are," she said. "Are you sure you want to go through with this?"

"I thought maybe you'd returned to town," I replied.

"Might as well," she said with a sigh, gesturing behind her.

Monitored by a surveillance camera and with a sign reading TRESPASSERS WILL BE PROSE-CUTED, Knott Grande's front gate shimmered in the shadowy fog. The motorized barricade blocking Kingfisher Street was the only passage through Knott Grande's barbed-wire perimeter.

In front of it, flopped like warm pudding poured on a plate, oblivious to the melee around him, lay Vesuvius.

"Should we let the dog sniff the sock now?" I asked.

"Only if you know how to open the gate," Georgia said.

"Hmmm," I said. "Let me think about this."

I sat down on a nearby boulder. Even through my thick denim jeans, it was warm to the touch. Thirsty from the ascent, I retrieved two cans of soda pop from my backpack and gave one to Georgia. Thinking he might like to stretch his several legs, I released Stony. Immediately, the little crustacean crawled into my lap.

"How's he doing?" Georgia asked, pulling the tab to open the can.

As innocent as her question was, it was destined to go unanswered. The pressurized carbonated beverage in her hand, having been thoroughly agitated during its travels in my backpack and heated by the prairie sun and volcanic earth, suddenly erupted, spewing a stream of thin, warm froth into my face.

"Dang!" I cried, leaping up to escape the assault.

This instinctive maneuver sent Stony tumbling from my lap, but I, distracted and temporarily blinded, didn't see where he landed.

"Gee whiz, Andy," complained Georgia, wiping her wet, sticky hands on her skirt. "How hard would it have been to buy cold ones?"

"They were cold when I got them, I swear," I said.

"Well, this one's empty now," Georgia grumbled. "Try opening the other one."

At this point, of course, I should have known better. If, under certain specific conditions, a can of gas-charged liquid performs in a particular way, the chances are extraordinarily high that another can just like it, when exposed to the very same conditions, will behave in an identical fashion. Such a reasoned hypothesis is at the heart of the scientific method. But just as the power of suggestion can get us to do things that we never thought of doing ourselves, so, too, can the power of instruction overwhelm our common sense, especially when that instruction comes from a strong-willed girl with a pretty face and a cheerleader uniform.

When I pulled the tab, cola shot from the can like a geyser.

And that's not all.

Stony, who only moments before had landed

unnoticed on the can, suddenly flew into the air, like America's first hermit crab launched into space. With a faint but disconcerting *ping,* the crustacean collided with the control box on Mr. Knott's electronic road barrier. Meanwhile, Vesuvius, intrigued by the missile whistling past his face, stumbled over to investigate, but as he reached the point of the hermit crab's impact, the old dog's wobbly legs gave out, and he fell against the metal obstacle like a sandbag. Magically, squeaking like a hamster in a wheel, the gate to Knott Grande slid open.

"Remember that combination," Georgia advised. "We may need it on the way back."

Mr. Farley, I Presume

In every decision we make, there is a point of no return. Time and time again, whether we realize it or not, we cross lines beyond which it's too late to turn back.

For Francisco Vásquez de Coronado, the decisive moment came when, leaving all but thirty of his men behind in what is now the state of Texas, he set off into the uncharted heart of the American continent to seek the gold of Quivira, a journey that ended in defeat and disillusionment at Mt. Mole. For Georgia, Stony, Vesuvius, Pegasus, and me, the destination was the same, but the scale was smaller, with the line defined by Mr. Knott's barbed-wire fence and gate across Kingfisher Street, where the terrain tilted up toward the mansion that once had been Coronado's castle. From this point on, even though natural forces were against us—gravity, grasshoppers, and whatever lies deep in the center of the earth—Georgia and I were committed to our fate.

Vesuvius, energized by a whiff of Mr. Farley's sock, astounded us by ascending Mt. Mole under his own power. Stony, once again secured in his terrarium inside my backpack, bounced out seismic warnings like a kangaroo on a trampoline. And while I clung to her from behind, Georgia coaxed the valiant Pegasus ever upward.

Although a champion without peer, Pegasus found the going tough. Several factors affect an electric scooter's performance: the freshness of the battery charge, the riders' weight, the angle of the terrain. Until now, Pegasus had known only the perfectly level streets of Mt. Mole. Now the stalwart scooter had a mountain to contend with, a natural speed bump rising to a height of one hundred and sixty-five feet—or possibly more. With two of us aboard, dodging rocks, swatting grasshoppers, you had to wonder—would we make it?

As it was, Pegasus and Vesuvius inched up the smoky mountain at the same lethargic speed, groaning side by side like competitors in a tortoise race. For me, standing atop Pegasus, the sensation was one

119

of riding in a very slow elevator, the main difference being that talking to the other passenger wasn't nearly so awkward.

"I get the feeling we're about to solve this mystery," I said.

"What mystery—Where's Waldo?" Georgia replied. "Who the heck cares? If Mr. Farley has any sense at all, he's long since hightailed it out of this hideous town. The mystery to me is why you insist on sticking around."

"I like it here," I explained.

"Excuse me?" Georgia answered. "I must have grasshoppers in my ears. For a minute there, it sounded as if you said you liked this godforsaken place."

"I did," I replied. "I have a good life in Mt. Mole."

"Andrew J. Forrest," Georgia said. "Take a good long look at yourself. You live in a third-rate motel. Your best friends are a mentally challenged crustacean and a battery-operated outdoor appliance. Your mother washes other people's hair to make ends meet. You've never even met your father. Your one escape from this grim existence is comic books. And now you and everybody you know are in danger of being blown to bits or toasted like marshmallows on a stick. Tell me, Andy, which part of this is the good part?"

"You left out that I recently met you," I said.

"Don't count on me, Andy," Georgia warned. "I'm

strictly temporary — just somebody along for the ride."

Suddenly, materializing through the smoke like a bogeyman, the dark, menacing outline of Knott Grande loomed in front of us. Vesuvius, perhaps from excitement, more likely from fear, began yapping loudly.

"We're here," I announced, hopping off Pegasus and taking a quick look around. "But where's the resistance?"

"The what?" Georgia asked.

"I was expecting armed guards," I explained.

"Great," Georgia said. "Now you tell me."

For as long as I could remember, I'd seen Knott Grande only from afar, a dreamlike fortification on a hill, at once mysterious and familiar — Mt. Mole's singular landmark. Up close, I found the renovated sixteenth-century castle to be even more imposing. Constructed on a greater-than-human scale in the old Moorish style, the four-hundred-year-old collaboration between Coronado and Mr. Knott left me feeling dwarfed, lost in the lengthening shadow of a soaring square tower anchored to a turret-topped wall of native stone aged to the color of moss.

"Where the heck is the door?" Georgia asked.

"Maybe it's on the other side," I said.

Barking like a puppy, Vesuvius was already on his way around. As Georgia and I followed, I was gratified to note that the wind had picked up and was now dispersing much of the mountain's veil of steam and smoke. The sun, descending into the horizon, had begun its brief, twice-a-day release of magic light.

From this elevation, the landscape went on forever, stretching out like an enchanted carpet at the feet of an ancient god. Decorated here and there by wildflowers flashing like tiny jewels, the prairie glowed as if made of gold.

What can I say? It was an incredible sight.

Here, I realized, were the long-sought riches of Quivira. Here was the legendary *montaña del oro* — the mountain of gold.

Some people see what they expect to see. Others discover surprises.

It's all in how you look at it.

For the longest time, I couldn't take my eyes away. Such was the vision's spell that I dared not move, fixed to the spot by awe and reverence. Only after a lingering, hypnotic period of open-mouthed amazement did I become conscious of Georgia at my side, holding my hand.

"This is beautiful," she whispered. "Absolutely beautiful."

"It's a true panoramic view," I observed. "You can see everything in every direction — all three hundred and sixty degrees."

To demonstrate, I turned my gaze toward town, a distant plaid square framed by First Street, Antelope,

Twenty-fourth, and Woodpecker. What I beheld was a tattersall tapestry sewn with golden threads, a work of art whose visible flaws — a dark swath cut by the tornado and a torn corner formed by the highway — only added to its loveliness.

But Georgia, it seemed, saw a different picture.

"Amazing how the view deteriorates when you turn around," she said, shaking her head. "Even from two miles away, that stupid, sad sack burg is still a dump."

Oh, well, I thought. *She's from out of town.*

In my mind, I imagined how Georgia and I must appear to Mt. Moleans watching from below — two tiny silhouettes arm in arm on the mountaintop, illuminated by a fiery orange sunset, serenaded by a deep prairie stillness.

That was when it dawned on me that Vesuvius had stopped barking.

That was also when I discovered why.

Miss Futon's elderly dog lay curled up at the feet of Mr. Farley, who was standing over a smoking hole in Knott Grande's front yard with a green plastic garden hose in his hand.

"Doggone it, Andy," he snarled, the right side of his mouth dragging the left side into a fearsome, Farleyesque scowl. "What are *you* doing here?"

A Summit Conference

Although obviously not a murder victim, nothing about the way Mr. Farley looked contradicted my theory that he'd been abducted and held captive for the past several days. Indeed, a second glance suggested he might have been tortured. For a man known to be obsessed with neatness, Mr. Farley was a sight to behold.

The once well-groomed assistant principal was dressed in a dirty blazer with missing buttons, a yellowed, sweat-stained shirt, and rumpled khaki slacks whose cuffs had been singed by fire. On his feet, he wore battered tasseled loafers encrusted with gray-white grime. His light brown hair, which he customarily combed straight back from his thick, black-framed glasses and Roman nose, drooped over his forehead in oily tendrils, like an upended bowl of yesterday's spaghetti.

Had I encountered him in any other setting, I would have figured Mr. Farley for a hobo, a wanderer, a boxcar-riding bum and not the exhausted would-be hero who stood before us trying to cool the overheated earth with a stream of tapwater.

"Well, no wonder you've been heading up the search party," Georgia said in a stage whisper. "Except for those hideous glasses, you look like him."

"Don't be ridiculous," I snapped. "I've known Mr.

Farley for years. Don't you think I would've noticed a resemblance?"

But even as I dismissed it, Georgia's observation triggered the sensation of always being the last to know.

"Andrew Jacob Forrest," barked Mr. Farley. "Go home! This is no place for children!"

Jacob? I thought. *Did he just call me "Andrew Jacob"?*

"We came for you," I said. "To deliver you from the clutches of Mr. Knott."

Mr. Farley's frown faded from his face, and for the first time I could recall, he smiled.

"You'd think that would be the goal of every resident of Mt. Mole," he said, "but those dimwits don't seem to know what a chokehold Uncle Lucius has on them."

"Uncle Lucius?" I said.

"Unfortunately, you can't choose your relatives," Mr. Farley observed.

"So you weren't abducted," I concluded, disappointed not to be carrying out a rescue.

"Actually, it was a very hasty summons," Mr. Farley clarified. "While digging into the mountain, Uncle Lucius cracked a natural volcanic seal. He thought maybe I could fix it."

"Can you?" I inquired.

"I don't know yet," Mr. Farley admitted.

"What was Mr. Knott trying to find?" I asked.

"Gold—what else?" Mr. Farley answered. "The old fool actually believed the legend. Look where it got him."

Through the fissure at Mr. Farley's feet, a plume of steam shot into the air. Instinctively, he stepped back.

"Where's Mr. Knott now?" I asked.

"Couldn't stand the heat," Mr. Farley answered. "Covered the hole with his dining room rug, then skipped town, leaving me to pick up the pieces."

"So you used the rug to make smoke signals," I deduced.

"Oh, you saw those?" Mr. Farley asked. "From where I was standing, I couldn't tell if they worked."

Mr. Farley twisted the nozzle, increasing the pressure of the stream pouring into the vent. I expected to hear a sizzle as the water flowed below the surface, but no such sound reached my ears. The passage into the center of the earth was bottomless.

"So, what's the verdict?" Georgia demanded, pointing to the hole. "Have you got that thing under control or haven't you?"

Mr. Farley laughed. "Nobody can control a volcano," he replied. "Not even a pipsqueak volcano like Mt. Mole. But I may have discouraged it for a while."

"Whew!" I exclaimed, stepping to the edge and peering into the steamy darkness. "That's a relief!"

"I wouldn't get so close if I were you," Georgia advised.

"It just goes to show what a difference one person can make," I said, ignoring my companion's girlish nervousness. "Especially when that person sets his mind to it."

It was just a simple pontification. Nothing more. A minor moment of well-meaning flattery, consistent with my character. But fate, it seems, took my remarks to be a heartfelt expression of philosophy — a proven dangerous act for me, one with serious, automatic consequences.

"What a difference one person can make," I foolishly declared in front of witnesses.

Few are our words worth remembering, even for a day. Fewer still are our utterances so profound we must write them down. But these words are branded into my consciousness forever. These words are fixed, permanent, like an epitaph carved by an artisan into a slab of marble, like a great truth recognized by all, like law, like wisdom, like holy scripture. These words were very nearly the last words I ever spoke.

"What a difference one person can make," I said, just before the effervescent earth belched, opened wide, and swallowed me whole.

"Good grief, Andy!" Georgia screamed. "What did you *think* was going to happen!"

Hats Off to Coronado

Upside down inside the dark crevasse, my feet reaching for the world I'd left behind, blood rushing to nourish the little-used capillaries of my brain, I considered my situation.

Amazingly, my descent into the abyss had been halted by my helmet. So seemingly impractical when first jammed on my head, the metal hat had proved itself a lifesaver when, point first, it struck an outcropping of lukewarm lava and stuck fast, like an arrow shot into a tar-covered road. If ever I'd wanted proof that life's great events are torn from the pages of Big Laff Comics, I had it now.

But what if this turns out to be the last page? I wondered.

I thought about the people I'd leave behind. Not just the ones you might expect, such as my mother or Georgia Wayne, but all the people of Mt. Mole. People such as Miss Futon, for example. How different my English teacher was when not in school, with her flower gardens, her pot of tea, her creaky old dog, and, curiously, Mr. Farley's socks. And Earl, filling his twilight years by operating a railroad between Mt. Mole and nowhere. And Mrs. Stitch, Miss Fleece, Reverend Oxide, Mrs. Bagelbottom, and the rest. As exasperating as they sometimes were, these people were like family to me.

Even the ones I didn't like, I cared about.

From far below came a rumbling sound. Steam hissed up the rocky chimney, tingling my nose and swaying me from side to side. But it was only the mountain breathing, a geological exhalation. I remained securely planted in the hardening ooze, helmet down and vertical, like ice cream pressed into a cone.

Farewell, people of Mt. Mole! I thought.

A tear fell from the corner of my eye, trickled through my eyebrows, and dripped onto the rocks, where it vaporized in a burst of salty steam.

Farewell Chief Eagle Talon! Farewell Fernelles! Farewell Mr. Knott! I continued.

I wondered if Jonah, trapped in the belly of the whale, had made a list of the people of his town. Is this what you do when you're alone in the dark and the end arrives? Who was I leaving out?

"Andy, can you hear me?"

The words sounded as if they were coming through a pipe.

"Andy, tap on a rock if you can hear my voice!"

It was Mr. Farley, calling from somewhere above my feet.

Of course! I thought. *I forgot to think about Mr. Farley!*

"I'm here," I shouted.

"Are you hurt?" he asked.

"I'm okay," I replied. "But I'm stuck."

"Hang on," he instructed. "I'll get you out of there."

True to his word, within minutes Mr. Farley lowered a rope, one that he'd tied into a cowboy-style lasso. After a couple of attempts, he managed to dangle it over my shoes, jerking it tight around my ankles. Now I was really in a fix, trussed up like a calf for branding, my head held fast at one end, my feet secured at the other.

What's next? I wondered. *Will I be stretched like a rubber band?*

It looked as if I'd have to risk it. With the hose removed to keep from drowning me, the rumbling sounds were getting louder, the vibrations were intensifying, and the air in the vent was becoming warmer. Time was of the essence.

The rope tightened painfully, but despite determined tugging from above, I didn't budge. My head was stuck in the helmet, and the helmet, it seemed, was cemented to the rock.

Eventually, as if Mr. Farley had given up, the rope went slack. Feeling returned to my throbbing feet.

Well, that's it, I thought. *It's all over now.*

I closed my eyes and saw all the residents of Mt. Mole assembled in front of me, like an audience standing in a sold-out theater, but instead of applauding or shouting "Encore," they were silently waving goodbye. From somewhere far below, the earth growled like an angry beast. In spite of the rising heat, I shivered.

Then I heard something, faint and far away.

I don't know how groundhogs do it. They must have very special ears. My sense of hearing was practically useless underground. Even ordinary sounds, like dogs barking or the prairie wind, were severely distorted.

At first, I thought the distant whir I heard might be the beating wings of insects, but when the rope around my feet became as taut as a string on a harp, it dawned on me that what I was hearing was the hum of Pegasus, as my stalwart scooter strained with all its battery-powered might to extract me from a premature grave.

Suddenly, with a *POP!* like a cork plucked from a bottle, my head slipped from Coronado's helmet, and I slithered feet first up the tunnel to freedom.

"Boy!" exclaimed Mr. Farley, clapping me on the back like a long-lost relative. "Am I glad to see you!"

"I'll say!" Georgia added. "I was sure you were a goner."

Our celebration, however, was short-lived. The volcano, angry over being cheated out of a human sacrifice, or simply overheated without its cooling tapwater fix, suddenly blew a gasket. Although mild by worldwide volcanic standards, the explosion sent a column of ash a quarter-mile into the air, obscuring Knott Grande, the mountain, and the three of us in a dark, foul-smelling cloud. Staggering, coughing, and groping in the smoke, it struck me that if I'd stayed in the vent a minute longer, I'd have been launched into the atmosphere like a bottle rocket.

Silently, I sent up a prayer of thanks.

"Andy, over here!"

The clear, compelling voice of a middle school cheerleader penetrated the deadly fog. With grasshoppers dropping around me like flies, I followed the sound and found an ash-covered Georgia standing with her right foot on Pegasus.

"Move back," I told her. "I'm driving."

"As you wish," she replied.

Mounting the scooter's platform, I clamped my hands around the handlebars and squeezed the speed control as far as it would go. To my dismay, Pegasus ignored the electronic command.

"Flip the switch," I instructed Georgia. "It must have gotten turned off."

Georgia dismounted and clicked the toggle on the motor. Then, to my surprise, she clicked it back again.

"It was already on," she reported.

"Are you sure?" I asked, as Pegasus again refused to start. "Many people get the 'O' and the 'I' mixed up."

"Well, I'm not one of them," she asserted.

"Dang!" I replied. "Then we must be out of juice."

"Well, we can't stay," Georgia pointed out. "This place is coming apart."

"Hop on," I ordered. "We still have wheels, and it's all downhill from here."

Beneath us, the earth rumbled and shook. Ash and steam shot up to the sky. Roasted grasshoppers drifted to the ground, their crisp, puffed bodies resembling popcorn on the floor at a matinee.

"Well," Georgia said, "what are you waiting for? Let's get going!"

"Not without Mr. Farley," I replied. "He's why we came here."

Over the creaks, cracks, and crashes of geological warfare, I screamed out the missing assistant principal's name.

"MISTER FARRR-LEY!"

"You're wasting your breath," Georgia announced. "He's out looking for Miss Futon's dog."

"How do you know?" I asked.

"He told me he was going to," Georgia replied, "once we pulled you from the hole."

To our left, something exploded as if hit with a mortar round. The shaking set my teeth to rattling.

"She's his girlfriend, you know," Georgia added.

"Miss Futon?" I responded.

"Yep," Georgia replied. "But if you ask me, I'd say he's still in love with your mother."

"WHAT?" I cried. "My mother? What gave you that idea?"

"He did," Georgia replied. "Come on, Andy. Why didn't you tell me Mr. Farley is your father?"

I looked at Georgia as if she'd shot me through the

heart. For the longest time, I didn't say a word, letting my mind drift where it wished in a long, strange, silent interlude during which night descended on Mt. Mole. Somewhere deep within the darkness, I could smell Knott Grande burning, I could hear its timbers crashing, I could feel its walls collapsing. Finally, having exhausted my willpower, I spoke.

"That's impossible," I declared.

But even as I said these words, I knew it wasn't. All it was, was that once again, I'd been the last to know, a situation Georgia dismissed with an unsympathetic shrug.

"We'd better go," she urged. "Time is not on our side."

"But, Georgia," I said, refusing to budge. "You don't understand."

Suddenly, emerging from the gloom like a stage actor through a parted curtain, the ghostly, gray-white figure of a man appeared. In his arms, he held Vesuvius, cradling the limp dog against his chest. Without saying a word, he advanced to where Georgia and I stood on Pegasus, lifted up his right foot, and placing a scuffed, tasseled loafer against the scooter's now-useless rear-mounted motor, gave us a mighty shove.

The Death of Pegasus

Whereas the journey to the top of Mt. Mole had been a leisurely lift in a freight elevator, the trip down was a toboggan ride. To say we flew would be an understatement. We shrieked down the mountainside like a jet with its afterburners on. Such a breakneck descent might have been thrilling under certain controlled conditions, say, as an attraction in a theme park, but this one was happening on a disintegrating mountain in the absolute darkness of nighttime and smoke.

Georgia and I hurtled through the harrowing void with nothing to comfort us but our screams. And though it was the fastest I've ever traveled by land, sea, or air, strangely, the trip down the side of Mt. Mole seemed to last forever. My entire life, all almost thirteen years of it, played before my eyes.

(Later, I calculated that the distance from the mountaintop to its base, before it leveled off at the two-mile road to town, was only two hundred and thirty-three feet. But at the time it was happening, mathematics was the last thing on my mind.)

Just as I was concluding that Pegasus had slipped off the edge of the planet and was plummeting through space, a light appeared. It wasn't one of those heavenly lights like the near-dead sometimes report, so radiant and intense that you can see even the tiniest object below, but a weak, shaky little light, indistinct and pale yellow, like a lantern in the hand of a very old man.

"Steer for the light!" Georgia hollered.

"What do you mean, 'steer,'" I screamed. "At this speed, the best I can do is hold on!"

"Well, slow down, then!" Georgia yelled. "Hit the brakes!"

"There's nothing left to hit," I informed her. "The brakes burned out a long time ago!"

As we got closer, the light grew larger until it resembled a spotlight like Mrs. Bagelbottom uses to illuminate actors on her stage. Reflecting off the smoke particles that swirled like midges in the air, it sliced a long, wavering, eerie beam right into our faces. It also emitted a low, mournful wail.

"Holy smokes!" Georgia cried, her shriek inflicting a sharp pain in my inner ear. "It's the train!"

Sure enough, behind the single feeble headlight was the Mt. Mole Society for Railroad Preservation's fully restored American Standard 4-4-0 steam locomotive, a twenty-five-ton iron and steel Cyclops, idle for more than fifty years, now bearing down on us at an unstoppable speed.

"Jump!" I commanded.

What followed was a tribute not to my athleticism, but to the human instinct for self-preservation. I leapt to port, tucked my head, and rolled across the ground, while Georgia conducted a similar maneuver to starboard.

Unmanned, Pegasus wobbled but plunged ahead, where it met the speeding engine broadside. Surprisingly, the impact didn't make a loud noise like a car crash, with metal brutalizing metal, and glass being shattered into grains of rice. Instead, it sounded more like a grasshopper crunched underfoot — just a slight, unnerving *pop* — hardly an appropriate finale for such a brave and faithful companion.

Perhaps the death of Pegasus was underplayed by choice. Perhaps my scooter understood that its role was only a supporting one. That night, the star of the show was the mountain. No sooner had the humble Pegasus laid its life down on the tracks than Mt. Mole responded with a performance so dramatic that no other mountain, no matter how famous or lofty it may be, can ever hope to top it. In a single, sudden instant, with a sound uniquely loud and horrible, Mt. Mole blew itself apart and disappeared, after which it began to rain.

"By the way," Georgia interjected as we watched the fallout from the mountain slowly turn to mud, "has it occurred to you that if you're related to Mr. Farley, and he's related to Mr. Knott, that you're related to Mr. Knott, too? No wonder you're always saying this stupid town is like a family!"

A Change of Scenery

Although they never became as popular as popcorn, Mt. Mole Mountain-Roasted Grasshoppers were quite a hit that year. It was Mrs. Stitch's idea to harvest the crispy husks from the carpet of volcanic ash, clean them, salt them, and package them in cellophane bags with a picture of the Fernelle twins and the words "two servings for the price of one." For a while, she had more business than she could handle.

She wasn't the only lucky one. While the eruption of Mt. Mole was forceful enough to reduce the one-hundred-and-sixty-five-foot formation to a rubble-strewn memory, no deadly lava flow followed the blast. So except for broken windows and a chronic ringing in the ears, the human population of Mt. Mole was spared from serious physical harm.

The psychological damage, however, is another story.

For Mt. Moleans, beaten down by tornadoes, drought, insect plagues, and the greedy, careless actions of its leading citizen, the loss of the town's only natural feature was the last straw. In the days following the great explosion, moving vans roamed the streets like taxicabs.

So many people pulled up stakes that I soon lost track, but among the first departures were Mrs. Stitch's sister, Miss Fleece; Mr. Knott's personal assistant, Luis; the reporter from the *Weekly Mountain*

Chronicle; nineteen members of the Mt. Mole Society for Railroad Preservation; two teachers and the nurse from Mt. Mole Middle School; the owner of Butcher Beauty College; the chef from the Knott Hungry Family Restaurant; the postman; the dry cleaner; the Tae Kwon Do instructor; the vice president of Knott Secure Savings & Loan; the landscape director of Mt. Mole Memorial Gardens; and the person at City Hall in charge of naming north-south streets.

"There's no work around here for me anymore," she said.

Such an exodus of essential citizens would be a hardship for any town, but to one as beleaguered as Mt. Mole, it was a catastrophe. And while I was saddened by the sight of each and every fleeing back, none affected me more deeply than the one I'd memorized while riding as a passenger on Pegasus — the spirited twelve-year-old daughter of Mr. and Mrs. Wayne.

In order to say our goodbyes in private, Georgia and I ignored the threat of another thunderstorm and took a long walk down Lizard Street, stopping when we came to the tracks. Although two days had passed since the mountain had vanished, the air hanging over the town continued to be hazy. So when I saw something shiny flash out of the corner of my eye, I focused on it right away. Hidden in the oil-soaked gravel of the railroad bed was a silver lug nut. I knelt down to retrieve it.

"It's from Pegasus," I said. "It's all that's left."

"This reminds me of the time we found that crab of yours," Georgia remarked. "He was about the same size."

I struggled to contain a sniffle.

"You seem to have trouble holding on to things," she continued. "Houses. Pets. Scooters."

I looked at Georgia closely. Her lips seemed on the verge of a smile, quite the opposite of my genetically ordained near-frown. When a wisp of blonde hair drifted across her forehead, she raised a downy fore-arm and, using her fingers as a wide-toothed comb, tucked it into place. There was no doubt about it. I was going to miss this girl.

"And people," I added, completing her list.

"I beg your pardon?" she asked.

"Nothing," I replied.

"Sorry I won't be able to see your play," Georgia said. "But my father says if we don't take that psy-chologist's offer, we could be stuck in this canker sore forever."

"I understand," I replied.

Dr. Blemish, convinced he was witnessing the real estate opportunity of a lifetime, was buying up a number of Mt. Mole properties, including the pile of splinters that had briefly housed the Waynes.

"It's too bad about Miss Futon's dog," Georgia went on. "Maybe if we'd tried laying him on his side and rolling him down the mountain—" Her voice trailed off.

Standing side by side, Georgia and I faced the space where the mountain had been. Far out on the prairie, a wispy curtain of gray lines extended to the ground. Rain was headed our way.

"I doubt that would have worked," I told her. "Vesuvius's time was probably up."

The sniffle that I was holding inside came rushing out. Continuing to watch the weather in the distance, Georgia reached her arm around my waist and gave me a sideways hug.

"Thanks," I said. "I needed that."

"I'm sorry about your father, too," she added softly. "Honestly, Andy, I don't see how you're holding up."

I wiped my watery eyes with my sleeve.

"I keep thinking things will get better," I explained.

In support of this point of view, the sun, hidden from us all morning long, peeked through the distant mist just enough to release a rainbow.

"Look!" I said, pointing.

A wide, multicolored band of light arced gracefully across the darkened sky, forming an iridescent outline the size and shape of the missing Mt. Mole. It was as if an invisible celestial artist were attempting to restore the view.

"Well, I'll be," Georgia said. "There's something you don't see every day."

"Yes, you do," I replied. "If you think you will."

"Oh, Andy," Georgia said. "You're one of a kind."

Then, to my astonishment, she kissed me. It wasn't one of those quick pecks on the cheek like you'd give to somebody so as not to hurt their feelings. This was a real grown-up kiss, right on the lips. She even closed her eyes when she did it. I know, because mine were open the entire time. That's when I saw the next amazing thing.

Beneath the rainbow, directly under the high point of the arch, a tiny, round spot was moving toward us, tiptoeing across the ground like a spider. While Georgia proceeded with her landmark kiss, I watched in fascination as the spot grew larger, until it took on the proportions of an old, fat, familiar dog.

"Please Georgia," I protested, when at last she surfaced to take a breath. "Not in front of Vesuvius."

Montaña del Oro

On the night of the performance of the middle school play, ticket holders were greeted with programs bearing the words, "Dedicated to the Memory of Jacob Farley, Citizen, Educator, and Father."

Confronted with the facts, my mother had little to add to what she'd already refused to explain.

"That was a long time ago," she asserted. "I've been trying to forget what happened ever since."

"But what about me?" I responded. "*I* happened."

"Well," she speculated. "That could be why I've been having so much trouble forgetting."

My drama teacher let me rewrite my soliloquy in the third act, an improvement that made the play run longer than anticipated. Standing center stage, a hatless Coronado faced the audience and proclaimed:

"I should have stayed in Spain. Oh, sure, I've been to places no other European has been, seen animals that would astonish a zookeeper, had adventures that no one in the Old World could ever believe. I've even found a mountain where no mountain ought to be. But I'd be a much happier man if I'd stayed where I belong. Is it too late to return? For now I know that the treasure I sacrificed my life to find was waiting all along for me at home."

Surprisingly, although once again I'd embarked on the personally hazardous subject of philosophy, the ceiling didn't collapse, nor did I fall into the orchestra pit. In fact, nothing much happened at all. But by then, the auditorium was less than one-fourth full, and many people — especially the railroad preservationists — had drifted off to sleep. When the curtain fell, only Mrs. Bagelbottom, my mother, and Dr. Blemish clapped loud enough for me to hear.

I didn't mind. I had the experience; that's what counts.

By the way, I don't believe that Mr. Farley's dead. The evidence — a living Vesuvius — supports this point of view. What I think Mr. Farley is doing at the moment is traveling. In fact, I wouldn't be surprised to get a postcard from him. Based on the photographs in his house, travel isn't just a hobby of his, it's a passion. To Mr. Farley, it would seem, home is just a place to hang your suits.

He may be my father, but we're not alike at all.

About the Author.

Richard W. Jennings is the author of *Orwell's Luck* (2000), *The Great Whale of Kansas* (2001), and *My Life of Crime* (2002), all published by Houghton Mifflin. He lives with his family in Leawood, Kansas.

MG 6/05

MLib

1/04